QUEEN OF HIS HEART

GAME OF LOVE SERIES BOOK 3

KHARDINE GRAY

QUEEN OF HIS HEART

Game of Love Series

Book 3

Khardine Gray
USA Today Bestselling Author

CHAPTER 1

Xander

TIME...

What time was it?

What time is it?

For a man who didn't have long to live I probably shouldn't be so obsessed with the time. What did it matter really?

It wasn't as if I could do anything. I was here, useless as shit.

Useless to everybody, including myself.

In my final moments I just wanted to think of her...

Jia...

Jia Marchesi, age twenty six, artist. Daughter of Giovanni Marchesi the Vegas Mafia King.

She was the innocent in the mix.

I was told that when I was given the mission brief.

Usually when we talked about innocents like that, it meant we weren't to involve them. As agents we weren't supposed to allow harm to come to them and most of all, we were supposed to be careful with them.

Be careful not to get them caught in the crossfire. Be careful of them getting close because the people we were targeting could sway them.

I broke every rule in the book with my innocent. I didn't just involve her, I got involved with her.

I got involved with her and it made me reckless.

It didn't matter now. I'd be selfish now and I could think of her for however long I had left.

I lifted my head and opened my eyes. There was a clock on the wall. I think Giovanni put it there to add to the torture.

I was attached to two metal pillars. Cuffed to them like I was in some risqué sex club, *fuck*, maybe that's what it was, some kind of torture chamber.

Giovanni wasn't the kind of man to like the risqué. But torture? Yes.

This apparatus I was attached to was definitely for torture. Torture to death kind of torture. Nothing more than that, nothing less.

The clock on the wall said it was three o'clock.

I just wasn't sure if it was three o'clock in the same day, three in the morning, or three p.m. the next day.

If it was any of the latter, it meant I wasn't thinking of her at a time when I knew she'd be thinking of me.

Jia.

She was going to Italy with Armand. She'd board a plane and fly off with him, out of the country. Far away from me. Far, so very far away from me.

I wanted to think of her at a time when I thought she'd be thinking about me. Boarding that plane. And looking out the window as it took off. That was what I imagined.

I imagined she'd cry and Armand wouldn't comfort her.

He'd leave her to cry for me. He'd hate her for it.

I hope she didn't cry because maybe he'd beat her for it. Or other things.

I wouldn't be there to save her.

If it was three pm the same day—Monday—then it hadn't happened yet.

If it was still Monday then that meant Giovanni would have been torturing me since last night when he captured me and I probably would have passed out a few times from the torture.

If it was still Monday then it would have been earlier that Jia came by and came through for me. She didn't talk. She didn't tell her father who I really was and that I came to steal from him. She knew practically everything about my presence here. *Everything*. Yet, she held her silence for me, just as she promised she would.

My girl came through for me and showed I could trust her, even when she watched me being tortured for the information and knew the torture meant death.

If it was still Monday then that's what happened earlier today.

Giovanni came to me several times after, to try and get me to talk.

Asking me the same questions over and over again.

Who did I work for?

Who sent me?

Who did I work for?

Who sent me?

I gave the same answer. I told him a fucking clown sent me. Granted he wasn't to know that in my rookie days of being a secret agent I thought of Ethan as a clown, because of the bizarre shit he used to ask us to do.

Fuck, I thought he was clowning around when he made Claire captain of our team and not me.

I thought it was a joke until he pointed out that my girl had more balls than me. Turned out he was right. I'd stopped thinking of him as the clown then.

But he'd become the clown again for the purposes of

today, if it was still today, because I wasn't dropping names.

I'd left Wes with two requests on what he should do if I failed in my grand plan to steal the blueprints. I asked him to tell Ethan what happened and then to tell Jia I loved her. That's what I asked him to do.

Whether or not it was still Monday, he would have known by now that I'd failed. Enough time had passed since Giovanni captured me to alert Wes to my failure.

I was supposed to message him when I got out of the secret chamber.

That never happened.

Wes would have known to take the next steps if he didn't hear from me.

It was so difficult to know what to do sometimes.

Sometimes when you thought you were doing the right thing. It turned out to be the wrong fucking thing to do.

In my case it always seemed like I was wrong whatever I did.

I thought by getting the prints myself I was going to be one step ahead of everybody. Not just Balthazar and his Spades, but everybody.

I thought it would give me an edge, something to work with and it would protect everyone else who was part of the mission.

Instead, I blew the mission out of the water and here I was. *Captured.*

Who knew what could be happening now?

Both Giovanni and The Chameleon knew of my presence, and they were so very far from stupid. Giovanni guessed right that I was an agent. He also knew I had to be of the special variety to disturb the nest.

I was pretty sure that global threat I was so worried about would come to pass.

Maybe...

There was always a maybe, but in this case I didn't know.

The situation was pretty bad.

The minute my mind started clearing up, a jolt of electricity ran through me and Giovanni's face came into my view.

Holy fuck!

I screamed. It was so fucking painful. So damn painful. Like a thousand knives piercing through my body. That was what it felt like.

Knives, swords, blades.

Pain beyond belief. Pain beyond measure.

They turned up the voltage again and administered another wave that made me heave like I was going to vomit. I was pretty sure I would have if I'd eaten. But there was nothing to come up.

Fucking hell.

How was I still alive?

Giovanni came right up into my face and snarled.

I'd foolishly thought he'd left me but he hadn't. Neither had the prick who was giving me the electric shocks. He was still very much here.

My ass was still being tortured. It hadn't fucking stopped.

Giovanni held up a hand and the electricity zapped away as it was switched off.

"Xander Cage, I'm growing tired of this. As you know I'm a very busy man. Very busy. I don't have time for shit like this," he taunted.

Fucking asshole. I didn't give a flying fuck about his schedule.

"Tell me what I want to know and this will be over. I'll kill you and you'll be dead. No more pain, son. Why would you prolong the torture? I never figured you for a man who liked pain. Come on tell me who sent you? Who sent you to steal my prints?"

The one fucking kick I got out of this was watching him squirm every time I gave an answer. It gave me strength to find my voice.

"A clo...wn. And, the prints aren't yours."

This time he didn't squirm, he answered me with a kick to my stomach that would have made me double over if I wasn't cuffed to the fucking pillars.

The pain from the kick and the electrical shocks were just too much. Once again I saw stars and felt my consciousness slipping.

Slipping away.

"You're a fool, you know that. I keep telling you you're the fool. Being used. Being fucking used. I told you The Ra wouldn't have gotten involved if somebody hadn't alerted them. Those prints are mine while they are in my care. The whole thing was covert. Oh so covert. *Shhhh.*" He pressed his fingers to his lips. "Covert and silent. I shouldn't have people like the Ra on my ass. No, and the Spades? Fucking hell Xander Cage. You know as much as me that mobsters keep their noses out of anything they don't belong in. No, no, no. We have enough wealth, but we still want more. Too dangerous, and we say no. We actually say no to things that are beyond us. This thing wasn't beyond me when I first agreed to it, then it became so. Like fuck."

He was talking out of his fucking ass. I wasn't sure if he expected me to feel sorry for him or, what his point was.

If I were even ten percent myself I would have told him to go fuck himself.

He leaned forward again and dropped a playing card.

The queen of hearts.

Jia. That was her.

She was the queen of my heart. The asshole knew what he was doing to me.

"It's fine. Play the game of silence, you fucktard. We'll resume this but rest assured, I haven't even begun yet to show you the extent of how truly evil I can be. Those shocks were nothing. That was just to try and crack the surface, but you refuse to cooperate. It's all good. *Ace*." He slapped my cheek and backed away.

He'd taken to calling me Ace earlier; assuming this was the same day.

"When you see me again, it'll be death and I'll take pleasure in killing your ass, but I'll make you suffer first. Maybe I'll cut your dick off for screwing around with my little girl, and I'll make you watch me kick it around in the dirt." He laughed then backed right out of my view.

Footsteps sounded then faded into nothingness. I couldn't hear anymore. I hung my head down and stared at the queen of hearts.

The image blurred into the ground and my mind drifted again. I drifted into the nothingness for what was likely hours. I didn't know.

It was more footsteps that woke me up. I blinked and geared myself up to see Giovanni again. He said he'd kill me. I didn't need any more pain. Maybe I would will myself to die somehow. Maybe I could just try to force my body to give up so it wouldn't have to go through any more.

The face that stood before me was not, however, Giovanni's.

It was Frankie.

Frankie, one of the knights. The only guy I could really say I got on with here. What would he do?

Had Giovanni sent him to kill me, knowing we'd been close to being called friends?

Was that what this was?

"Kid, boy I wished you'd listened to me. They messed you up bad," he remarked. Despair clouded his russet eyes as his gaze assessed me.

My lips parted but I couldn't talk. My throat was so dry and my body weak.

But... not too weak to take note of what he did next. He pulled out a key and moved to undo the cuff on my right hand.

"Get this side Vin," he instructed, glancing over his shoulder.

Surprise took me when Vinny stepped forward and took hold of my right side, holding me up so I wouldn't drop to the ground.

In the meantime Frankie unlocked the cuff on my left hand and took hold of my left side. Both of them supported me. I looked from one to the other, not quite sure what they were doing yet. These two guys after all, were Giovanni's most trusted people. His capos.

"What ... what are you doing?" I asked weakly.

"What the fuck does it look like we're doing, prick?" Vinny threw back.

"Just don't talk." Frankie told me. "Here to rescue you from shit. *Capisce?*"

I couldn't believe it. *Jesus.*

"*Capisce,*" I answered.

CHAPTER 2

Xander

THE TWO CARRIED me out back. When the night air hit me, it hurt all over.

It was night again so a whole day had gone by. I forgot to look at the clock.

Was it the same day?

They put me in the back of Frankie's truck but Vinny didn't get in.

Frankie got into the driver's seat and Vinny came up to the window.

"You asshole," he said to Frankie. "You better know what you're doing. He'll kill you when he finds out."

"I'd like to see him try," Frankie answered with a daring smirk, cocking his head to the side so the light from the lamp post beamed down on his black spiky hair.

Vinny sighed with an uneasy expression, tensing his square jaw. His hawk-like eyes switched from Frankie to me, then back to Frankie. "I'll hold the fort here."

"Hey," Frankie shook his head and held up his finger. "You know nothing, and you never helped me. I'm serious. This is on me. My sister won't be without a husband."

Vinny dipped his head understanding and backed away into the shadows of the night.

I barely managed to keep my eyes opened as I looked at him. Frankie drove off, leaving him standing there.

I bid him a silent thanks.

I struggled to keep myself up. It was so hard. All I could manage to do was slump against the seat.

"There's a sweatshirt in the back next to you. Put it on," Frankie instructed. "There's also a bottle of water. Drink some."

I swallowed hard against my dry throat. The lump there was so big it actually felt like I'd shoved a ball inside and was trying to move past it. Very similar to having a sore throat, or when I'd had tonsillitis. It was so bad, I'd needed my tonsils removed. Thank God I'd had Jack in my life then, because it crippled me for weeks.

I was thanking God and his heavenly host now that I had Frankie. And Vinny? Fuck...

What the hell?

Frankie had watched my back over the last few weeks, giving me a pass to see Jia. If not for him I would never have had the chance. I never expected this though. Not from him and definitely not from Vinny.

Pulling in a deep breath I gathered strength to straighten up. The hooded sweatshirt was folded next to me, the bottle of water under it.

My arms were like lead pillars as I lifted them up to shrug into the shirt. Then I downed the water, my throat thanking me in abundance.

Jesus, it actually made me feel a little better. I must have been severely dehydrated.

Frankie's eyes alternated between watching me and the road ahead.

I stared at the back of his head and he glanced around at me.

He was definitely help that had come in the most unexpected form.

"Thank you," I told him. "Thank you and Vinny. But Jesus, why? Why did you do it? Giovanni will know someone had to have helped me."

Giovanni would have known that straight off the

bat when he discovered I was missing. He knew I had skill but there was no way I was that good.

Frankie was silent for a few seconds.

"I helped because we're in over our heads in something that I never signed up for. Vinny helped because we've always watched each other's backs and he gets married to my little sister next spring. He's family. It's what we do." He gave me a little smile.

"I get it, but there's more, right? What do you think you're in over your heads with?" He'd helped me but I needed to be careful with what I said and what I revealed.

I was slowly getting my mental strength back. Protocol would suggest that as soon as I could move, I should get in touch with Wes and Ethan.

Protocol at the moment was bull shit to me, with all the variables I had to wrap my head around. I was more inclined to take a different approach and gather more intel. Not just act like I was used to acting.

Also...

Here I was acting like an agent but I wasn't that. I might have been hired by Ethan and the Special Missions Forces, but I wasn't an agent.

I didn't have to think about protocol.

"For some time I've sensed something more than the usual going on in the background with Giovanni. More than what we do as gangsters. I'm all up for money but there comes a point when that line of reason has been crossed. He always does those high stakes games. Months ago I saw a guy linked with the Cuban Cartel and I heard whispers of selling something to the biggest buyer Giovanni had ever had. I didn't get a name but... I knew the level of shit was serious. Political. Government related and not ours."

A shiver ran down my spine.

When this thing all started, it was clear as the days unfolded that there were several players involved.

Giovanni was in league with The Chameleon, an illegal black market trader. *And,* Diego Sanchez, a notorious member of the Cuban Cartel. I'd bet Diego was who Frankie saw Giovanni with.

Giovanni had stolen blue prints from a military envoy. The blueprints were a design to build a nuclear weapon unlike any known to man. Those people: Giovanni, The Chameleon and Diego were all facilitators, working for someone else. My team and I were not sure who. But we assumed they were working for someone terrorist related. We never factored in that it could be government related. We never factored it in and we were too busy dealing with the other side of the madness which was that Balthazar and the Ra, were after the blueprints. Better to say Balthazar and the Ra because as I'd seen for myself just last week he didn't just have his Spades with him. There were ordinary Ra guys helping out like worker ants, furthering the cause.

There was so much at work here. Too much.

Trying to process too much at once was hurting my brain.

One thing at a time... Frankie said government.

"Which one Frankie? Which government?"

"I think Russian. I don't know for certain. The thing that got to me the most was the secrets. Giovanni sent in the four knights who were killed to steal something. The rest of us were not privy to knowing what the something was." He glanced back at me again.

I'd come to that conclusion on my first day at work. It was when I knew I'd have to go looking for the blueprints old school. I'd assumed my job would have been to watch over the blueprints but then quickly realized the remaining knights didn't have a clue about them at all.

"Why didn't he share the details with you?"

"Giovanni is a very particular man. He has his host of men protecting him and his assets like an army. The knights however get chosen for different things. Vinny and I are muscle. Armand the closest to him is an advisor and *consigliere*. Freddo is business minded. You would have been chosen for your keen attention to detail and ability to outsmart him. You were what was needed I guess in an emergency. The other four were what I call ruthless bastards. They used to run a ring where they stole all types of shit. Giovanni classed them as his generals. They were the guys who went above and beyond. If he wanted something done, they'd do it and leave no trace. We were all shocked to shit when we heard they'd all been killed."

It was their deaths that opened the position for me. Except Giovanni didn't have four replacements, he just had me. It was my skill. From the beginning he was always impressed with it and my attitude. I sufficed for what he needed, which was mainly to watch the casino and keep my eyes open for trouble. He had the others watch Jia, especially when he found out we were involved.

"So, back on track, why did I help you? Several reasons. The first was I think you came to steal the thing we don't know about, also kid, you stuck out like a fucking sore thumb. I thought straight off the bat that you'd been sent. You aren't a cop, and you aren't military either. You're not clean enough to pass for that shit. Those guys move differently." He cleared his throat. "I'm not about supporting terrorism or pitting government against government. That's above me. What's more above me is groups like the Ra. I don't know a lot about them but when I realized they were involved, I was out from then. Out in every essence of the word."

"When did you know they were involved?"

"The night of the shootout, kid. We got rid of the bodies of the guys who came for us. Giovanni ordered us to take them to his crematorium. When I was prepping the men I saw the tats that linked them."

I nodded. "The Ankh."

"Yes, the fucking Ankh."

The general members of The Ra had a tattoo of an Ankh on their wrists. The Spades also had that in addition to a tattoo on their cheeks of a spade. Balthazar was their leader, however, to my knowledge he did bear any of the marks that distinguished his faction or The Ra as a whole. He was his own monstrosity of a person.

"Not everybody knows what it means," Frankie pointed out. That was pure truth. The Ra were a secret group and you had to travel in some special government or underground circles to even know of their existence. "Vinny sure as hell didn't and neither did Armand. I don't think Giovanni thought we'd have any idea. He never thought I'd know. That bastard didn't even have the decency to tell us what we were dealing with. He just assumed we were dumb as fuck. And, he still hasn't said. Any extra is what I gathered from what he said to you as he tortured you."

"How do you know about the Ra?

"Let's just say I hear a lot of things I shouldn't in the underworld. I see even more things. I knew what the tattoo meant. It could only have been them that killed the other four knights. Right from then though, I suspected a rat. A fucking rat. Seeing the tat told me hands down that there was definitely a fucking rat amongst us and I think it's that prick Armand."

Armand...

Jia had mentioned something about him. She said she saw him meeting with someone and it looked off to her. Hearing Frankie say this now was even more reason for suspicion.

"Armand, why do you think it's him?"

"He's shady as shit, Xander. I don't know how you can ask me that. He's the only one of us with that lack-adaisical attitude. He has a get out of jail card on account of his ties back to Italy and connections to the Marchesi family. It means it gives him more freedom than the rest of us to move around and do stuff."

The night of the shootout Armand was screwing around with one of the maids. But, he didn't have to exactly be around at the same time the Ra guys came in. They could have already been there waiting.

"He has access Xander, and that means a lot in our world. I can't figure it all yet, but I suspect that son of a bitch. He's the only guy who knew who would be at the poker games. All the players taking part and guests. Granted anybody who has deep pockets can attend and play, but the point is he would have had some idea who was coming. I think he's working with someone else. The fucking web goes deep. Tangled up in knots so tight I can't figure it. Giovanni is right though."

"About what part?"

The man had said so much.

"He said The Ra would only get involved the way they are if they were tipped off. I didn't know the specs of whatever the four knights were stealing but it was secret enough to keep it right under wraps. No one should know about Giovanni's involvement at all."

Ethan had said one of the guys was caught on camera. That was how the SMF knew. If Armand was working with the Ra, he could have tipped them off. It didn't fit though. Something didn't fit.

There was someone else.

Again, like Giovanni said, the someone was the joker. A person who'd managed to fool everybody and get all involved on this wild ride.

I thought he was right about that.

"So you think Armand squealed?"

"I think he squealed for the right price. I think he's in balls deep for the right price. It actually grieves me that Jia has to have anything to do with him. The other reason I helped you was her."

Just the mention of her name gripped my heart.

"I hated that she saw me being tortured."

"Me too. Giovanni is one ruthless son of a bitch, but

fuck, he definitely used to take the premise of keeping women out of business to another level. If this was another time he would never have allowed her to see something like that. It's no excuse. The bastard is in over his head and acting out because of that. He won't take me down with him when the shit hits the fan." He gave me a more quizzical look, one more of scrutiny. "So, I won't ask who you work for. Take you from the frying pan to the fire. All that shit. I reckon if you held your silence for so long and endured the torture Giovanni put on you, it must be important. What I will ask you is this. You one of the good guys?" He held my gaze through his reflection.

I nodded. "I am. I came with good intentions to stop bad from happening. Only bad can happen when certain things fall into the wrong people's hands."

"That's good enough for me. Can I ask what the thing is? This thing it's all about, that you came to steal. Is it okay to ask that?" He gave me a tentative expression. "I wasn't able to really hear what it was while Giovanni was torturing you. I heard the word 'prints' drop, but couldn't really tell with all that was going on."

I didn't see any harm in telling him that part given the circumstances. Or, rather clarifying. The issue of what it was I was here to steal wasn't the worry anymore. It was what would happen next. Frankie seemed to know enough and some of what he'd shared with me was more than I knew before my sketchy plan to steal the prints went to hell.

"Blueprints for a nuke," I replied, pulling in a deep breath. "A super nuke with a combo mix of uranium and plutonium. They were designed by a scientist at NASA."

His face hardened and he looked back to me. "Fuck, you're serious?

I nodded.

"Fucking hell, I was right. I was fucking right. I knew it was serious but I didn't know it was that."

"It's serious." And I didn't have the damn prints. The mission was blown, The Chameleon saw me too, when he and Giovanni caught me with the prints in my hands in the chamber.

They could have moved the prints by now.

Now... when was it?

I got that disoriented feel again of not knowing what day it was. That made me think of Jia.

I gazed out the window, at the shadows of night.

I was too afraid to ask what day it was. It was something I needed to ask though.

"Frankie, what day is it? Is it still Monday?"

He smirked. "Kid they must have really did a fucking number on you."

Fuck. I prayed weeks hadn't gone by or something like that. I really was out of it and displaced.

"Frankie I'm serious. I just want to know for her. For Jia. She gets on that plane with that bastard."

Understanding filled his eyes in the reflection. "I get it. It's still Monday. Her plane leaves in two hours."

Two hours.

Oh my God. She hadn't left yet. She hadn't left with Armand yet. I straightened up even more and for the first time since getting this mission to get the prints, I wholeheartedly thought of what I wanted most.

I had a second chance to try.

"Frankie, I appreciate the rescue. I do, but I have to get her. I can't let her go off with Armand."

He chuckled again.

"Yeah, I figured as much. I also thought you'd need a ride to make that happen. Gotta say though kid, that you don't look like you can move all that fast so you probably need all the help you can get."

All I could do was stare at him.

"What are you saying to me? You gonna help me?"

"Where do you think we're going?"

I swallowed and the lump loosened in my throat. I glanced out the window again and saw signs for McCarran International.

CHAPTER 3

Jia

ARMAND WAS SITTING across from me in the limo.

He gave me the occasional glare of annoyance. It was the type of look to kill.

It was the type of look that told me to be careful, be wary, be aware.

I just didn't care anymore. He could kill me for all I cared.

He could just kill me, and if he didn't I just might do it myself.

I was sure death was better than this.

This... me heading to Italy with a man I'd hated almost as much as I hated my father.

How did I get to this point?

How did I get here at this point in my life where I practically had nothing? Not even my God given right of choice. How could I be a grown woman of twenty six years old and be going through this shit?

The car careened down the road. We weren't far from the airport now.

Another twenty minutes tops and we'd be there.

We'd fly by private jet at ten. I hated flying that way, usually for the company. Today would be the worst time.

It would be so much worse because it was just going to be Armand, me, the flight attendant and two pilots in the plane.

Just days ago Armand tried to rape me and here I sat with him enroute to Italy to be married in two weeks.

Yup.

That was my life. that was what I had to look forward to and worse, I had to do it knowing my father had killed the man I love.

I didn't know if Xander was already dead, or if he was still alive. I didn't know. I was assuming death. If he was still alive I figured it would only be a matter of time. He looked.... bad earlier.

That was a little over eight hours ago. He'd looked

bad then and I didn't think with all that I'd seen being done to him that Xander would last past the next hour.

It was so awful.

"Your thoughts are deafening *bellezza.*" Armand suddenly snapped, cutting into the silence. His voice took on an edge that pierced through me.

It made me tremble. I guess it didn't help that I was crying too, he would have hated that.

"What do you expect? Do you expect me to be as heartless as you?" I countered.

"I expect you to forget that prick and focus on the future. We're getting married in two weeks and here you are bawling over your dead lover."

Dead?

Christ it was true. Armand had confirmation. He'd spoken to Pa several times throughout the day, maybe he got confirmation that Xander... died.

God, no... please.

I shuddered inwardly hoping against hope that it wasn't true.

"You know he's dead?" I asked.

He leaned forward and grabbed my face. I winced when he pressed his mouth down hard against my lips and kissed me. When I didn't kiss him back he bit my bottom lip, squeezed down with a force that made me scream, then released me. I grabbed my mouth, shaking from the pain.

Although tears poured from my eyes, I raised my hand and slapped him hard across his cheek.

My retaliation, however, did nothing. It was nothing to him.

Completely unfazed, Armand just smiled at me.

He held his face and beamed at me. "Love the fire baby. Can't wait to get my little slut in bed." He gave me a deep hearty chuckle. "I hope Xander is dead. Forget him Jia. Forget. *Him.* You are trying my patience and you know patience is not one of my virtues."

"I wasn't aware that you had any virtues Armand," I spat back.

He leaned forward again. "I'd watch that tongue of yours Jia. I own you now. I own your sexy as fuck ass. If you want to have a decent life I would definitely watch what you say to me."

I laughed a laugh without humor and shook my head at him. "Armand, threaten me all you want, do whatever you want to me. You people are fools. Don't you realize that you and Pa killed the only leverage you had over me. You're basically telling me Xander is dead. So you think you own me, you only *think* you own me. But, I'm just a shell. A body."

He smiled and his gaze dropped to my breasts, lingered there for far too long, and climbed back up to meet my eyes.

"I'm very happy with the body Jia. Very happy and

I'll take it," his viperous tongue uttered, making me sick. Everything about this man made me sick. Sick like I'd vomit, especially when I thought of having to sleep with him. I knew I'd have to whether he forced me to or not. It would happen.

"Do you really have no form of decency?"

"No. I do not. I simply exist and take what I want *bellezza*." He touched my face and ran his finger down the length of my neck, down to my chest and over my right breast, brushing his finger backwards and forwards over my nipple.

I cringed and his grip tightened on my breast, the touch becoming a clasp.

I winced, recoiling from him but he pulled me back.

"You're hurting me, stop it." I gasped. "Armand stop."

"When will you tell me yes? Your lover is dead. When will you say yes to me? You used to."

Every time I was reminded that I used to be with this man I died a little inside. He wasn't like this. Not at all. The power Pa had given him went straight to his head.

In the past he would never have laid a hand on me and he knew the word no meant no. He would never have forced himself on me or touched me when I didn't want to be touched.

That was the past and I suspected I was naïve and

lacked awareness to see him for who he was until the day I caught him cheating on me.

"I will never say yes to you Armand. Never. I don't know how you could be okay with that. You'll have me, but I will never love you. I will never give myself to you. You will be the loser."

"I'm not the loser here, it's you. You couldn't leave well enough alone. Not my fault that you got caught up in shit and burned, you were told what was expected of you and you went against it. The only person to blame in a scenario like that is yourself. Not anybody else."

I couldn't answer.

I couldn't give him any form of comeback because he was right, he was actually right.

I got involved with Xander and there came a point where I should have ended it but didn't. I should have ended it when I found out who Xander was. I couldn't resist him though, then I fell for him. He had me hooked right from the start. The only result was this.

I looked away from Armand and he released me.

I gazed out the window, out to the shadows of night, out to the lights that lit the approach to the route that would take us to the airport.

It was better not to think about it, better to go through the damn motions and take each minute as it came. My problem was I was still hoping. I was praying. But there was nothing to hope or pray for.

We got to the airport in the time I'd guessed.

Pa was waiting for us.

Frankie was standing next to him and Freddo. Frankie was a welcomed sight. He'd been nice to me over the last few weeks.

I needed nice and he'd made it possible for Xander and I to see each other.

Pa greeted Armand in the usual way. I couldn't believe it though when he came to give me a hug and a kiss.

Just this afternoon he'd treated me as little more than a rag doll when he shoved me onto the balcony and tried to get me to rat on Xander.

He was acting now like nothing had happened.

Like this was some meeting we always had and he was simply seeing me off.

"Everything okay?" he asked Armand.

"Everything is perfect and ready to go." Pride danced on Armand's stupid face.

"Wonderful. Is there anything you two need?" Pa's eyes glittered with the satisfaction of this moment I still couldn't believe was happening.

I was at the airport. I was actually here walking through the motion of this nightmare.

Armand shook his head in response and I just stared

back at Pa, blank and expressionless. I just stared at him and stiffened like a statue.

Pa set his eyes on me and he narrowed them. "Jia, a little less tension from you would be appreciated."

"Did you kill him?" I asked ignoring his shit comments. "Is he dead?"

Pa looked uncomfortable at the question, but he did that usual hard man thing by trying to look like he didn't care. The thing was, I knew he didn't care about Xander. What he cared about was what I thought about him. He cared that I'd stopped looking up to him.

"My dear girl, it is time to stop thinking about our enemies. Time to move forward and focus ahead."

"Did you kill him?" I repeated, ignoring his bullshit. As far as I was concerned Pa was everybody's enemy. He got involved with the wrong people and this was a symptom of that.

"He will be dead before the stroke of midnight I'm sure. If not, a bullet to the head should do the trick."

I bit down hard on my back teeth and gave him a long hardened look of despair.

"I hate you," I seethed. Resentment burned my chest. "I hate you."

My father had done a number of things in my life, all enough to make me hate him. It was because of him, him with his enemies, that my mother died. They came at her to get to him. It was his fault. He'd done enough questionable things. Despite that, never once had I told him that I hated him.

Not once.

From the rage in his eyes and the line etched across his jaw, I could see my words stung.

"That's okay my love. You can hate me if you want to, that's fine. It happens just like shit. It happens. You simply don't understand. That is all. I can't expect you to fall in line with everything I say. But at least I know I got to keep you safe and with someone who can do it." He looked from me to Armand.

I needed… some space.

God… I needed space. Lightheadedness and tension took me from the angst of everything.

Some time away from them was what I needed, even a minute to breathe.

"I need … two minutes." I panted, running a hand through my hair which was now a matted mess.

"What for?" Pa flared.

"Please, I just need two minutes and then I'll come back. The ladies room. I just need to go."

"I'll go with her," Frankie offered.

I swore Armand was just about to say the same thing but he was one of the people I needed the much needed break from.

I was relieved when Pa nodded his agreement.

Frankie stepped forward first and started walking. I followed next to him.

Once we got a little distance away from them he set an arm around me and I found myself leaning into him for support. Support and comfort.

"Frankie I can barely walk, I feel like I'm dying." I tried to stave off a fresh bout of tears.

"Princess, I need you to not die on me right now. I need you to have a little more strength just to get out of here."

I lifted my head not quite following what he was saying to me.

"Frankie, Pa's going to kill Xander..." my voice trailed off.

"No. He won't. Don't worry about Xander."

I wasn't sure how he could tell me that when he knew Pa was serious. We all saw today that Pa had every intention of killing Xander.

"I'm worried sick and I feel like I'm going to die if I step on that plane." My voice shook as did my legs and he held me closer as I stumbled.

"Calm doll," he leaned nearer to my ear. "Lucky for you, you won't be getting on that plane."

I tensed and shuffled to face him as we walked but he held me still, tightening his grip around my waist.

"Don't," he broke in quickly with a rasp. "Just walk with me and act normal. Please."

God, my heart...

It raced a hundred miles an hour. It galloped.

Was this hope? Could I hope?

Frankie was the only person among Pa's knights who would have known that just being here was killing me inside. He was the only person who knew how I felt about Xander.

He would have known that me stepping on that plane meant me signing my life away. It was death. It would be. Nothing else could describe it better than death. Death to my body and soul. All that was left of me.

Jesus please... Please let this be hope.

We went down the escalator and continued to the signs for the toilets. We went through the section and he went into the ladies division with me. The custodian on duty went to say something to Frankie, but one hardened look cast his way and the man backed down without a word.

Frankie was the kind of man I wouldn't have wanted to mess with either.

We walked the whole way down the cubicles and headed to a door that said staff only.

He moved his hand away from my waist when we got there and took my hand instead.

He walked faster and I followed.

I followed and my brain caught right the hell up. I caught up to what we were doing, what he was doing.

We went through the door and the night air graced my skin.

Frankie didn't falter in step, he kept going with me, pushing forward ahead in a straight line, never looking back.

We verged on the parking lot and I saw his truck. It looked like someone was in the back.

"Princess, jump in the back seat as quick as you can, now," he ordered, letting go of my hand. We ran to his truck and he headed to the driver's seat. I did as he instructed and jumped into the backseat.

As I did my eyes landed on Xander.

He was there.

I'd barely registered that this was real, and it really was him, before Frankie gunned the engine and took off at lightning speed out of the parking lot in true mobster style.

"Xander," I gasped when Xander reached forward and touched my face.

His hands were shaking, but it was him. His face was a bloodied mess. Dark, dark circles were under his eyes and he was completely messed up.

"Baby," he replied and rested his head back on the seat.

QUEEN OF HIS HEART

I slipped my arm around him and held him. He felt so weak in my arms.

Yes, Pa was right about him being close to death. He looked like he was on the verge of death.

Only God knew how my man must have suffered.

"Baby…" he whispered on the edge of a breath.

"I'm here." I assured him and looked to Frankie who was looking at me through the rearview mirror.

He did this. Frankie saved Xander and they came for me. They saved me.

"Frankie thank you so much," I told him. A tear spilled down my cheek. "Thank you so much Frankie.

"Jia, girl we're in for one rough ride. I'm just letting you know princess. Just letting you know. Your father will not take this lightly."

I nodded. "I know."

CHAPTER 4

JIA

MY SENSES HEIGHTENED the minute Frankie's phone went off. They were already on high alert from the second I felt that Pa would be looking for me, that was half an hour ago.

Frankie answered the phone. I thought it was Pa calling but it was Vinny.

Frankie had the phone on speaker.

"He just called me man. The boss just called me. Wants to know if you've been in touch. He's looking for you and Jia at the airport. I said I haven't heard anything," Vinny blurted.

It sounded like he was in on this plan too.

"Good. I'm gonna get gone with them."

"Fuck man, he'll kill you I know it."

"Yeah, he'll try to. See you on the other side bro. Don't call me again, and dispose of the phone. I don't want you linked to this in any way."

"Understood brother. I'll do what I can from this side." Vinny hung up.

Frankie focused on me and glanced at Xander who'd fallen asleep in my arms.

"We have separate phones. Your father would have tracked me if I used the phone he has the number for," Frankie explained.

"I can't believe you're doing this. He'll know it's you," I winced, swallowing hard.

"Yeah I know. I might have gotten away with getting your boy out because that whole area has no surveillance whatsoever, but I knew I was all in balls to the wall when I knew I had to come get you."

"Thank you." I couldn't say thanks enough.

"Not just me princess. It's him. You were the first thing on his mind when he realized he had a chance. Nothing else. The goal is to get the fuck off the radar. Giovanni has his empire of people and they have eyes. Cops and criminals alike. If I can get us out of sight then we can get ahead."

It sounded like he had a plan.

"Frankie what are we gonna do? Can we really just disappear?"

"I hope you guys can. I want you to. The boss still has the thing Xander came to get. *The blueprints.*" He said that in a way to let me know he knew.

"The blueprints?"

He nodded. "He still has them and while he does it's not good. I won't be able to just get back inside so I don't know what's going to happen on that front." He gave me a poignant stare. "I think it's best we take one thing, one step at a time. Get off radar first then think about the other stuff after."

I agreed. That was definitely in order.

"What can I do? I have to do something to help."

"No, Jia. I know through this whole thing you hated being told what to do, but I'm gonna need you to do exactly that. This is out of your league. There's some people we'll head to in San Diego. I reckon we can hide out there for a max of a day or two. We get there and I hide the truck. Your boy needs to heal. He needs to heal something bad. Don't be surprised if …" He paused and the linger of silence worried me. "We just have to hope your father didn't drain him out too much. That whole setup was designed to kill him. The last guy… well, fucking hell, the last guy that was attached to the torture chamber blew up. The voltage was too high."

I sucked in a sharp breath. "Oh my God."

"Yeah. He came to kill your father and that was how your father got him to talk. Guy gave a name; your father got the person who ordered the hit but he still killed the guy for fun. Set the fucking volts to blow the bejesus out of him and that is exactly what he did. Xander was just a few volts away from that and he was whipped. I'm hoping there was no internal damage."

I gazed down at Xander in my lap. He really did look injured. Pale and weak.

"We should take him to the hospital. Frankie we can't let him die."

"Can't go to a hospital Jia. There's a doc at the place I'm heading to. I'm hoping they can fix him up. I'm hoping we can get him fixed up because honestly I don't know what we'll do after. We got to get out of the state. Get fucking far away. He wasn't able to tell me about his people. You know anything about who they are?"

I did but I wasn't sure if I should say.

"Can I tell you Frankie?" My tone told him it wasn't really a question on whether or not I could. It was a matter of *should*.

He tilted his head to the side. "Doll... okay fine. How about we talk when he wakes up. Would that be better?"

"Yeah, I just don't want to feel like I betrayed his

trust. That's all. I trust you though. I do. Please don't think I don't."

"I know you do, it's why I'm here." He held my gaze. "You know everything, don't you?"

I drew in a breath and nodded slowly. "Yeah."

"You knew and you kept your silence. That took some serious balls Jia, it seriously did. And with your father…I'm proud of you for doing that. You chose the right thing."

I bit back the wave of emotion that came over me. Hearing that I did something right was so uplifting. It truly was.

"That means a lot Frankie, it really does. It's very rare that I'm told such things, very rare. You know on this occasion I had to choose Xander."

"Yes, doll, I know. It made me think. If you could stand up to the boss and do the right thing, I could too. Your actions did not go unnoticed."

I remembered how he'd looked when I walked into the castle courtyard earlier today, and I remembered through my tears how he'd looked as I was carried away from Xander.

I knew he'd noticed what the whole thing did to me, but I hadn't realized he'd seen deeper.

"I think for the first time I truly realized how evil Pa was," I stated, blinking back tears.

No one, no matter who they were could be so easily

accepting of the fact that there was so much darkness in a person they were supposed to love.

A parent.

Pa had turned my love to hate. Nevertheless, it didn't make me hurt any less. It didn't ease the depth of disappointment in him.

"My dear you have no idea. I'm guessing since you know a lot I can share this with you," He focused ahead on the road. "Something feels off Jia. Giovanni was really concerned with who hired Xander. I don't think it was because he wanted to simply get a name, it felt more than that."

"What do you mean?"

"Just a feeling *bellezza*. It occurred to me from the way he tortured him, he would have just killed him. I think he would have done. I've worked for your father for nearly twenty years. I know the man. I know him and know that he doesn't pussyfoot around shit for no simple reason, asking the same questions."

"I understand. So you think what?"

"I don't know, that's just the thing. I don't fucking know. What I feel now is that Armand is definitely in cahoots with The Ra."

Okay, he'd said Ra. I could talk about them.

"A man from the Ra came to my home yesterday. His name was Balthazar Kane. He's a leader of sorts –"

"I know who he is Jia." He cut in and glared at me.

"Fuck, this just keeps on getting better and better. That is not a name that is thrown around lightly, nor is it one to trifle with. Didn't fucking know he went to your house. *Fuck.*" He hit out at the steering wheel.

A shiver ran through me just watching him.

Christ. I knew to be afraid from yesterday. Balthazar had someone with a rifle trained on me. The last time I'd felt fear like that was when Ma was killed. I'd been seconds away from death. Yesterday was like that, knowing I could be dead before I drew my next breath.

"Frankie, he said he knew I was Xander's weakness. He killed... he killed Xander's girlfriend."

Frankie paused for a few seconds and looked to me. "This is not good Jia. Not good at all. Armand is involved, but he's just a pawn. A guy like Balthazar wouldn't have gone through someone like Armand. He wouldn't and we can't have a guy like that on our ass as well as your Pa."

"What do we do?"

"I pray your boy wakes up with some ideas. He's no mere person either. That did not go unnoticed by me at all. Tricks up his sleeve and secrets. I can tell."

I looked at Xander and again I agreed.

Pa said to me the other week that I didn't know much about him, even after all that had happened I still didn't know as much as I'd wanted to.

All the same, I still loved him. I knew his soul and it

was enough. I fell in love with his soul. That was enough to love him.

Even so, we'd reached a point where I needed to know more.

I needed to know more because I wanted to help.

One hour passed and we pulled off the highway.

All around us was desert land.

It was just a dark expanse of nothingness, reminding me of something from the set of one of those films where one of the characters breaks down on the road and then ended up stranded. Then some kind of a serial killer would take her, kill her and bury her somewhere in the expanse. Nobody would find her.

Sounded like I might have watched one too many films, but when that was your life and your father was like mine, it wasn't all that hard to imagine. I couldn't claim to have seen it happen but I knew stuff. I would be very foolish to assume the stuff that happened in the movies was just reserved for just that.

Pa had a cleanup crew that came on the scene when they needed to clear bodies.

My first experience with the like was after I watched my mother get killed and seconds later my father shot the man who killed her. Donny Morales.

That was his name and he was, in those seconds, getting ready to kill me too.

Pa killed him, saving me.

Part of me always remembered that, even though Pa locked me away for months after the incident happened. He locked me away to keep me safe. It was horrible but for my safety.

All that time though, I never knew what it was Pa had done to Donny to make him come for us in that way. I still didn't know.

The cleanup crew took him. A year later I saw on the news that the feds found body parts in the desert. Not even all the body parts. A hand and a head. That was it, and it was of course a skeleton of the hand and head. They were able to establish that it was Donny. The other parts of him were never found.

I knew what had happened to him, and I knew only one person could have arranged for him to be disposed of in such a way.

We turned off the road sharply and it snapped me out of my thoughts.

Frankie and I hadn't said all that much in the last hour. Xander shifted and groaned like he was going to wake up but then drifted back off to sleep.

"We're practically there, doll," Frankie declared.

Ten minutes later we approached a woodland area with a lake. The moonlight beamed down on it in that fairytale manner that made the water sparkle and glisten. It was the sort of picturesque scenery I would have loved to paint. Definitely loved to paint something so moving yet peaceful with the overpowering silver moon hanging over the lake and trees with a shiver of shadows surrounding it.

Something for another time, maybe.

My creative mind was always seeking something, desperate to do what it loved. That was what I should have been doing.

This started out with me just wanting to go to Europe to finish my art studies. That was all.

Then things changed.

We drove for a few more minutes until a cottage came into view.

I gazed on ahead, curious.

We parked up and the door to the cottage opened. A woman rushed out. She looked like a classical image of an Italian mother. Warm presence, plump, long wavy hair that flowed out into the night and when she got close I realized she looked like an older version of Frankie.

"Ma," he beamed and she smiled.

Frankie got out and gave her a hug.

I'd never heard Frankie talk about his family. All the time he'd worked for Pa he never mentioned them. I understood why. It must have been that same thing of keeping the people you love out of business.

Two men rushed out of the house too, both looked like him also.

Brothers maybe.

While his mother helped me out, the guys got Xander.

We all went inside. Xander was placed in a room where one of the guys tended to his wounds. He worked like a doctor so I guess he had to be exactly that.

I stayed with him while Frankie went off with his mother.

I learned within minutes that the guy tending to Xander was Alberto, Frankie's middle brother and the other guy was Zivelle. He was the youngest.

I observed them as they moved around and I could tell they were separate, as in they seemed to exist outside the business. Outside the usual mafia related restraints. It was their mannerisms that gave them away.

Alberto had a lot of work to do on Xander. He had broken ribs and thankfully that seemed to be the worst thing that we could tell just from the physical examination he did on him.

He did advise us to go to the hospital though as soon as we could because there was no telling what damage could have happened internally without more extensive checks.

Of course I definitely agreed. It was just on the basis of a matter of when and how we would get to the hospital.

Xander woke up fully a little while after but he was so weak. We had him propped up on a stack of pillows. I sat next to him with a warm rag placed on his head that seemed to comfort him. He'd complained of a headache earlier.

Every time it went cold I'd warm it up.

I was just about to again when Xander reached for my hand and pulled me back to sit down.

"Baby..." he breathed.

I moved to him, careful to avoid his wounds and kissed him. It was a kiss my body longed for. "Xander..."

"Jia." He cupped my face and it was a direct contrast to the rough manner in which Armand had handled me earlier.

When Xander touched me it warmed my heart.

"How are you feeling?" I moved my hand over the edge of his jaw.

"Can I just be happy to see you?" His voice was thick with emotion.

"Of course."

"Stay with me, just stay here. My head feels fine. I

don't need that rag anymore. Just you."

I cupped his face too, looking over his bruises. I couldn't believe I was holding him. "Of course. If you need me to warm it again in a little while I will."

He smoothed his hand up my face.

"I love you," he told me on the edge of a heartfelt whisper. His words were like a gentle caress on my soul.

I beamed down at him. "I love you too."

"Thank you."

I chuckled. "You aren't supposed to say thanks."

"Baby… it would only be bad if one of us told the other they loved them and the answer was thanks." He gave me a weak smile.

"I know, that's really bad. But I mean you don't have to thank me for loving you."

He bowed his head for a few seconds then lifted it back up, his bright blue eyes meeting mine. "I do… I do, because I trust you. I trust you, Jia, with everything I have in me. I don't find it easy to trust people. You have proven to be the most trustworthy person I've ever met in my life."

He was talking about this morning.

"It's okay. I told you I wouldn't say anything," I reminded him.

"You could have though, I'm not sure that if the tables were turned that I could have done what you did.

I've never been placed in such a situation and it was unfair that you were. I slipped up baby and I got caught." His hand dropped like a leaded weight to his side.

"Can you talk to me a little more about what's going on? The blueprints I mean, and what happened when Pa caught you. Do you feel strong enough to talk?" It was my eagerness to help taking over. Seeing him so helpless made me want to help even more and do what I could, whatever that may be. It was like I'd found strength from somewhere despite the weakness that had taken me earlier while I was with Armand.

"Yes... The blueprints are for a nuke... and your father was keeping them in a place where he didn't share with his knights." He seemed a little more stronger as he spoke, although he took a few breaks to catch his breath. He swallowed hard then continued. "The area was all secret. No surveillance, not even on the plans for the building. My friend, his name is Wes, he always had my back. I thought it would be safer for me alone to go for the prints when some Ra guys jumped us at our base. So I went alone, blind and your father caught me. You know the rest of the story."

"God, Xander. I'm so sorry. I knew it was supposed to be goodbye and all I could do was imagine what you must have been doing. Xander, my father still has the prints. What do we do about that?"

He pressed his lips together and stared at me.

"Nothing. There's nothing I can do. Jia he wouldn't be foolish enough to put the prints back in the same place, it's a given. Do you remember at the poker game that night? You asked me about a man that was there?"

"Yeah, Russian looking guy."

"He's a black market trader. We also call him The Chameleon because of how he vanishes in plain sight. My advantage that night was that he'd never seen me before. He however caught me along with your father and it was always the worry in my team that if he got the prints then that would be it. We wouldn't know what happened to them. I'm guessing he has them now."

Great...

"So, there's nothing we can do?"

"There's only one thing I'm going to do and that's take care of you." He looked at me with firm determination.

I would have loved to feel happy about the declaration but fear got the better of me.

It really did.

It also switched my focus from the prints to the more pressing problem, my father.

He always said I was the most important thing to him. I believed him.

I believed him and I expected the whole Marchesi clan to be after us by morning.

CHAPTER 5

Xander

I SENT A MESSAGE TO WES.

Nothing in the content. It was blank.

It was a signal to let him know I was alive.

I was alive and would contact him as soon as I could.

That was the gist of the message.

Blank for safety reasons.

The same sort of message was sent to Ethan. For him it was a code though. Code 9. Meant the mission had been compromised and he should move to the next plan of action. Whatever that was.

Whatever it was wouldn't involve me and I supposed I'd be in the shitstorm I'd been in previously, back to square one.

I sent the code to confirm the next steps even though I'd left Wes with the instructions. I guessed Ethan would have probably taken action anyway, given shit hit the fan days ago, nevertheless, having confirmation the mission had been compromised sealed the deal.

I'd managed to get myself up and emailed him the code, blotting out the IP address so it couldn't be traced here to Frankie's family.

I didn't say where I was because this place wasn't for me to broadcast.

Frankie hadn't said anything to me to caution me, but I guessed straightaway that he'd kept his family away from his life and activities with Giovanni.

The way they carried themselves was a dead give-away. They were different. Not so tense or on edge. We'd been here for a day and a half and it felt like living back in Idaho with Jack.

I grew up rough in Chicago. That was where he found me and took me in. A year later he moved to the farm house in Idaho.

I'd thought he was going to bid his goodbyes when he told me he was selling up and moving. Then he said he wanted his kids to have some of the country life like he had. Kids, as in plural. Claire and me.

It was then that he really became family to me.

Knowing that he would not only take me with him, no questions asked, but also he made sure he got a big enough place so that I had my own room and space in abundance.

He wanted me to have somewhere I could call home and always return to.

Neither of us knew at the time that I would end up falling for his daughter.

These people here lived like him, so it wasn't for me to give my location away.

Like Frankie, Wes and I had separate phones. My phone had been taken from me but I'd memorized Wes' number for the secret phone.

He'd messaged back with the same blank message. That meant received.

I was sitting on the edge of the bed trying to heal my core. I did some deep breathing techniques I'd learned from some Buddhist monks in Nepal.

The technique helped to build inner strength. As soon as I got mine we needed to make a move.

On my plan I wanted us gone by morning. The early hours of the morning, so we'd still have the cover of darkness.

Frankie came into the room and looked me over with concern.

Another thing I'd done when I got some ounce of

my strength back was talk to both him and Jia properly. I gave them the full run down on me.

I'd felt they deserved it. They more than deserved to at least know me given that they'd risked their necks for me multiple times and we were in the height of it. There were no secrets now. I'd filled in all the blanks and even told them about Claire and Jack. They knew that to everybody else I was supposed to be dead and that just got wiped from my records so I could blend in when I became a knight.

Frankie had that same expression he held then. One that offered compassion and understanding.

"Hey." He grinned.

"Hey there."

"You look stronger."

"Must be the food." I managed a smile. Frankie chuckled.

Jia was with his mother, cooking. Earlier they'd gotten talking about food. Jia being such a great cook and lover of fine cooked meals got sucked in straight away, right into the conversation and then ended up heading off to make some classic Italian dishes. She'd come up with lunch earlier and it was divine.

"I'm not gonna disagree. It's heaven being in a house with two of my favorite cooks." Frankie made his way over to me and sat on the edge of the bed. "How you actually doing buddy?"

"I'm trying to get stronger. Mind and body. I was thinking we should get gone by morning. Maybe four or earlier. Grab some sleep, then head out."

"I'm cool with that."

My shoulders tensed. "Frankie, I meant me and Jia."

He gave me a cunning smile. "I know you're healing yourself up so you can get back in bed with her as quick as possible, and you probably want your privacy, but I'm coming."

I laughed. It hurt to laugh but it was worth it. It was moments like these that lightened the tension.

"That's not why. You've done enough for me, you've done enough for Jia too." He had done more than enough, his help was... well I couldn't have done it without him. Not one damn bit.

"How can it be enough when your journey's just beginning? Who knows what the hell Giovanni must be going through. He probably thinks I'm the rat in the circle and I kidnapped his daughter and handed her over to The Ra." He chuckled.

It wasn't funny. It was a possibility that Giovanni could think that but I'd be the wild card in the mix.

"He won't. Because he'll know you helped me, he'll know this is a separate problem. But he'll go crazy nonetheless. I've never met a man like that before, love and crazy mixed together. I get that parents do what they can for their kids but he's just..." I didn't quite know what to call him.

"*Bad*," Frankie filled in.

"I don't know if that's the right description. I'm bad."

"You're a fucking badass. There's different levels of bad. Some of it isn't all bad. That's why I knew you couldn't have been a cop. Play too dirty. That day you nearly killed Armand spoke all. You messed that mothafucka up real bad. Gotta hand it to you. I could see you would have done it though, because of what he was going to do."

That was the day Armand tried to rape Jia, it was days ago.

"I snapped because I hate abuse of power. Preying on the weak. Abusing the weak," I explained.

"So, that makes you not bad then. So that's why I'm coming with you. I think you need the help Xander. If you guys go I think I'd worry, plus I don't really have much of an alibi."

"What about your people here? Your family?"

"I keep them out of business. I didn't want my younger brothers involved. No one knows about them except Vinny, but he rarely comes here, for safety reasons. My sister is a nurse. She works in the city. He sees her there."

"What if Giovanni comes for any of them?"

It wasn't like it couldn't happen. It was highly likely.

"Can't think like that Xander. But if it comes to that I'll call for backup in Chicago. My cousin is the boss there."

"Boss of Chicago?" I knew Giovanni considered himself the Vegas King. It could have been the same. Of all the mobsters I'd known Giovanni was the most flamboyant. The others didn't tend to broadcast themselves or their wealth the way he did.

"You heard me man. Boss of Chicago. Claudius Morientz and his brother, Lucian is just as bad as him. Giovanni thinks he's hot shit because of his success, but there's worse than him. Giovanni knows I have Chicago and anyone who knows the relation knows not to come for me. Within reason. I won't make the mistake of thinking I'm immune or that shit won't happen. It's more of a deterrent. As in I think Giovanni will do everything he can before he comes for me through my family. My family is their famiglia too. You don't want to piss on Chicago."

I didn't doubt him if he said so.

"I hope it won't get to that stage. We just try to do whatever we can, which is?"

Here's where he wanted to have the plan.

"My family. He's like a father to me, but we aren't related."

Jack.

He was my idea for now. I knew the only person

who could help me now was him. We'd get to Idaho and
I'd have something to work with. We'd have a place to
stay and hide out. A place to think and I could contact
Wes.

"Where is your *would be* father?"

"Idaho."

Frankie frowned. "Well at least we'll totally get
gone. What about the prints Xander, don't you want to
try and get them again?"

I shook my head. "Mission's blown. There's no
point. It took me weeks to work out where Giovanni
was hiding them. He would have handed them over, I
think to one of the people he was working with. I think
he would have done that."

"You *think*? But we don't know for sure."

I nodded. "I'm ninety percent certain. I think The
Chameleon would have taken them."

He pulled in a deep breath. "So we just run?"

"Yeah. I think so. I sent my people the code to let
them know I'd failed. I'm hoping they'll find another
way. I don't know. I just need to get Jia somewhere safe.
Somewhere that doesn't jeopardize your family. By the
way I didn't give my location away to anyone."

"I appreciate that." He stood up when the door
opened and Jia poked her blond head in.

She smiled when she saw me sitting up and floated
over to me.

"I'll leave you two. See you later." Frankie smiled and left us.

Jia sat next to me and I placed an arm around her.

"You're sitting up." She beamed.

"I'm sitting up and I feel stronger. Much stronger," I assured her.

She ran her fingers over my chest. The slight touch stirred that need for her I always had just from the sight. All I had to do was look at her and I wanted her.

"It's so good to see you like this." Her beautiful eyes sparkled. "I made cannelloni. I couldn't help it, it'll be ready soon."

It was good that she could keep occupied with cooking so she wouldn't worry too much. I for one knew she was terrified.

"Sounds amazing baby."

"Is there anything you need?"

"You." The answer was true and simple.

"I'm here."

"Kiss me."

She crooked her finger and beckoned me to come to her delicious lips for a kiss. I was only too happy to oblige and taste her sweetness. Sweet like honey but she had that element of something that made her more desirable. It was passion. Hot sexy passion that cut through to my want for her, even in my weakened state.

She was my weakness in every way.

CHAPTER 6

Jia

I WAS TRYING to be positive.

I figured that was the best way to help. Even if it was nothing really.

Being positive helped keep up morale.

It made me worry, however, of what would truly happen in the long run.

I took out my phone from my bag, so tempted to switch it on. It was Anya that was on my mind.

I wondered if maybe I could have done something similar to how Xander contacted his friend. I very quickly abandoned that idea though because it might put her in danger. I knew what Pa was like, he would check everything and leave no stone unturned. That was what he would do.

He'd go to her and question her. He'd check out all her stuff to see if I'd made contact. One thing I hoped he didn't do was hurt her in any way.

That would have killed me. Just thinking of that happening, through all the shit I'd seen Pa do over the last few weeks, which I had to class as his worst moments, I felt he wouldn't involve Anya more than necessary.

I put my phone back in my bag and quietly made my way back to Xander's room.

It was super late and everyone had gone to sleep.

When last I checked it was just after one in the morning and we needed to be up in a few hours to leave.

I probably shouldn't disturb Xander but I just wanted to check on him as I was up then I'd leave.

Maribelle, Frankie's mom, had given us each a room. She'd guessed quickly though that Xander and I were involved from the way that I cared for him and talked about him. My room had been the closest to his.

When I opened his door I expected to see him in bed, lying down asleep, but the damn man who should have been at the very least resting, was on the floor doing pushups. The moonlight that beamed through the window lit him up, making him look like some kind of warrior in prep for war.

Of all the things... I couldn't believe my eyes when I saw him going for it. I was a gym bunny on the regular and in what I classed as my normal days, but I doubted I could have done one push up the way he was doing it by pressing on his knuckles. Much less the amount he'd done in just the few seconds I'd stood there.

He stopped and gazed at me with the sexy half smile, looking a lot closer to his charming self than he had in days.

His dark blond hair was ruffled with that just-got-out-of-bed sexy edge and to add to the image of him, he stood shirtless before me with just the bandages wrapping around his washboard stomach.

"You come to watch me?" he asked keeping his voice low.

"You're supposed to be in bed," I chided.

He smirked again.

I went in and closed the door.

I gave him a little smile when he switched on the desk lamp.

"Try sleeping when you have to come up with a master plan."

I moved closer to him and his gaze dropped to my breasts.

"Try sleeping when your girl looks like this and she's

in a different room to you," he added, looking me over with seduction.

Maribelle had given me a nightshirt to wear. It caught my legs but because of the deep V neck it made my breasts look bigger. Or more enhanced.

He'd noticed.

"Again you should be resting." I giggled, trying to keep as quiet as I could.

It was hard and I wasn't sure how thin the walls were. Frankie's room was down the hall.

Xander got closer and reached for me, bunching up the shirt and pulling me flush against him. The lift of the shirt exposed my black lace panties, making him smile. He pulled the top higher and nodded with satisfaction.

"Miss Jia you sure are a great sight to heal the injured," he remarked and bent low to place a kiss at the edge of my hip.

I swatted his hands away when he pulled me closer and tried to kiss me when he straightened.

"No." I shook my head. I could feel it.

Passion's call.

I could feel it filtering through the space between us and tempting me. I remembered how well it didn't care where we were or what state we were in. When it came to claim us it came full force and brought along its friends: desire and wild pleasure.

"No to what baby?" He got to me and tugged on the shirt again.

"I know what you're thinking. It's in your eyes and I'm only here to check on you. You need to rest Xander."

He moved closer and turned his smile up several notches. "I need you."

That had a very different feel to how he'd said it yesterday. "You're wounded still and you should be sleeping."

"Don't you want to help me feel better?"

I gave him an incredulous glare. "Yes of course." Then I gritted my teeth and spoke in a low whisper. "Xander we can't have sex here."

Not the way we did it, definitely not the way we did it. We were that couple who needed to be far away, or at least somewhere where the walls were thick.

"We could be really quiet. Like mice, except sexier. Quiet."

I smiled when he reached for me again. The touch of his fingers on my bare skin as they fluttered over my cheek made me warm to the idea.

Quiet... We could be...

Damn it, I was thinking about it even though I shouldn't. It would be so embarrassing if someone did come to check on Xander and caught us having sex. Then again, there was something more arousing at the thought of trying to have sex and keep it quiet. Something forbidden that made it appeal to me.

"What if I hurt you? You're injured Xander." The fact that those words slipped from my lips and went past the part of my brain that was still trying to process meant I'd already decided we were doing this.

He gave my body a full sweep and his eyes darkened with molten heat. "I was doing pushups baby. Believe me this will be a lot more fun, plus how the fuck do you expect me to let you go, with your tits looking like that?"

He smoothed his hand down to cup my left breast and moved the fabric across to expose the soft, ample flesh. Both my nipples puckered on their own just from his heated gaze.

By the time he ran his finger over the tips they hardened right up, almost painfully.

"It's been too long since I touched you," he breathed and lowered to cover the diamond-tipped nipple with his hot wet mouth.

Oh my God, I couldn't believe I'd tried to resist. That felt so damn good it made me wet instantly. He sucked hard and I moaned from the pleasure and instantly covered my mouth, stifling a giggle when he lifted his head and placed a finger to his lips.

We were so bad.

I backed out of his grasp and pulled the night shirt

over my head leaving just my panties on. I really hoped no one else came in to check on Xander.

He slipped his arm around my waist and scooped me up to carry me over to the bed. He'd picked me up like I weighed nothing and like he hadn't been on the verge of death days ago.

It was only days ago that I nearly lost him.

Thinking it saddened me. It dimmed the sexual desire that coursed through my veins and I cupped his face.

"Don't you fucking dare stop me." He warned with a sexy chuckle. "We can totally be quiet."

I quirked my lips. "I know. I'm just looking at you."

"Watch me do this."

He propped me on the pillows and bent his head down to resume his sucking. From one breast to the other he sucked and licked, giving me unimaginable pleasure I'd only ever experienced with him. Working the tips to life he aroused me to that point where I could have screamed into the pleasure but I held off by clamping my hand over my mouth. The devil looked up at me and smiled that wicked sinful smile he knew would get me good and it did too when he caught the end of my nipple in between his thumb and forefinger and the light pink nipples darkened.

Fuck, that felt so good. It felt so good and I couldn't

resist the little moan that slipped from my lips. It wasn't loud, just low enough for us.

He parted my legs and pushed his finger deep inside my pussy. His smile widened when he saw how wet I was.

"Yes. Good girl, wet and ready for me." He whispered and kissed his way down to my mound where he added another finger and started finger fucking me.

I wasn't sure how the hell I was supposed to keep quiet when that felt so damn good. Then Xander being Xander, god of pleasure and giver of fantasy orgasms, had to amplify his movements by moving his fingers faster in my pussy while he moved up to suck my right breast and massage my left nipple with his free hand.

He sucked in the same rhythm he moved his fingers. Fast and pleasure filled, giving me exactly what I'd craved.

No it was more. Pleasure everywhere, all over.

The greedy orgasm that took me was ruthless in every sense.

There was nothing tame about it. It just came. It came and I arched my back into the pillows to cry out but he moved to my lips to swallow the cry.

Instead of the tell-all pleasure cry that would have woken up everyone in the house, it came out like a muffle. A strangled muffle that made my whole body flush.

He stopped his speed and pulled back from my lips to stare down at me.

"Sorry, maybe I shouldn't do that," he breathed.

"It was amazing. Why the hell did you choose tonight of all the nights to do that to me?" I giggled.

"Maybe I want you more, and I always want you." He glanced down at his fingers still in my core, pulled them out and licked them. He licked his fingers like he was enjoying some exotic dish and seeing him do that pulled at my groin.

"Fuck, you taste so good. I need more Jia." He growled and parted my legs wider.

No fingers this time, I knew what he was going to do and I wanted it bad. That meant I'd have to be quiet on my own.

He nuzzled his face in between my thighs, thrust his tongue deep inside my pussy and started licking.

Licking and lapping up the nectar that had flowed out of me then licking around my folds, then licking at the already swollen nub of my clit.

That was when the tug of need came again. Pleasure in pure rawness clawed its way from deep within. Clawed its way to the surface of my skin and brought with it fire that singed and scorched me clean.

A hot wave washed over me, bathing my body in the wild buzz. Making me crave and enjoy everything he gave me.

QUEEN OF HIS HEART

This time when orgasm number two took me I tensed up and blew out the breath so I wouldn't scream into it. That made me shudder and writhe against him as I came again.

I moaned but it was loud. Not enough to worry over, but it seemed to arouse him. He sucked harder, drinking and lapping. Taking everything, wasting nothing.

He looked up at me and saw the shudder that took me, making my breasts bounce.

Xander moved up to me to suckle again, taking the left breast this time and sucking until the shudder ceased.

When it did, he slipped off the bed and shrugged out of his pants and boxers, unleashing his massive cock. It seemed bigger tonight.

In the warm glow of the soft light from the desk lamp and the mingle of the moonlight he was a masterpiece. The light outlined all the perfect parts of him, which was everything. Muscles on muscles, his tattoos and even his bruises and scars. All of it was perfection to me.

All of it called to me.

The godlike man crawled back on the bed. Slid my panties down my legs and took hold of his cock.

I always liked watching that part. He'd hold it like he was trying to calm himself and exude some level of control. What was better was it was all for me.

He was all for me.

Guiding the fat head of his cock to my entrance, he rubbed against my folds to tease me open, then thrust into my pussy. The length and thickness of his cock filled me right up, searing into me like he was branding me. Always making me his.

I couldn't believe we almost never had this moment again. It had come so close. Like something minor could have changed the outcome. Something so small could have happened to take him from me.

He inched in deeper, hitting my g-spot. The effect was so powerful it wiped my brain clean. It robbed me of what I'd been thinking and everything.

Nothing mattered but the emotion, nothing mattered but pleasure.

It was only once he started moving inside me that awareness snapped back to me when the bed started rocking and creaking against the floor.

He pumped a little more and a little faster and shook the bed, but didn't stop.

Before I could say anything, he pulled out, picked me up and set me on the floor in the center of the rug, on my hands and knees.

He gripped my hips and I glanced over my shoulder.

The wicked smile on his face told me he wasn't about to hold back.

"This way I get to fuck you properly." He said that more of a promise.

I believed him.

He plunged in again and fulfilled his words.

We'd made love before but this wasn't that, it was something else entirely.

His relentless thrusts that built up and seemed to rise with each pump sent me over the edge, feeling so good in this position. When he started fucking me hard and rutting into me with the power of the pleasure, I had to stifle that scream again. My hair fell forward over my face and my breasts bounced painfully in front of me.

It was like we'd both gone wild and lost our minds.

I sucked in a sharp breath to cool the cry that would have torn from my lips. At the same time that he squeezed my hips tighter and pounded home, jackhammering into his release.

I was already over the edge, my end just pushed me further and sent me into the arms of ecstasy. It severed me in two. Snapping me in half and then into several little pieces.

All pieces of me that luxuriated with pleasure.

God... my skin...

Fire...

My skin...it was on fire and the heat made me lightheaded.

Xander ran a hand over my back, down the curve and lingered there. The touch was so gentle and in contrast to how we'd been just seconds ago.

He pulled out of me and pulled me into his chest, flush against him, our bodies wet with sweat. I turned into the corded muscles of his chest but he cupped my face and gazed into my eyes.

"Be mine Jia... when this is over. Please be mine." His eyes lightened now, another contrast to the heat that had filled them.

"I was always yours Xander Cage," I replied.

That made him smile. "Thank you, I'm glad to hear it because you had me at hello."

CHAPTER 7

Xander

A knock sounded on the door. It was a light tap.

It woke me up but realistically I should have been awake already. Although my body felt stronger, I was still suffering from the effects of the torture.

The tap sounded again, more cautious this time.

It was Frankie. He opened the door and poked his head inside.

"It's three fifteen. Didn't know if you wanted to get up early and get something to eat," he said.

"No, I'm still full from the ten course meal your

mom gave me." I smiled groggily, straightening up and focusing on him. My movement made Jia wake too.

He chuckled when he saw her. "That's alright man. I'm gonna go get the truck ready."

"Thanks, I'll be down soon."

"Cool." He tipped his head and left us.

According to my plan we had forty five minutes but honestly the sooner we left, the better. We'd just get to Idaho quicker. It was gonna be one hell of a drive. It would take us the whole day. I counted around fifteen hours with stops for breaks. I knew I'd feel better once we got out of state.

Jia straightened up and moved to kiss me but pulled back.

"What? No." I reached for her.

"I am not kissing you with morning breath. Ughh, and must you look so gorgeous. You're supposed to be injured. At least look like it. I look like I woke up in a barn."

I didn't know what she was saying to me, she was the one who looked gorgeous with that platinum blond hair cascading down her shoulders in long graceful waves. When she tried to slip off the bed I pulled her back and planted a kiss on her lips.

"You have gorgeous honey breath," I told her, loving the feel of her in my arms. "And you look sexy, just-woke-up-in-my-arms sexy."

I could easily get used to this. Definitely get used to it.

Not now though.

We had things to do.

She backed away and looked me over. "How are you feeling? *Truly*. I shouldn't have come in here. I should have allowed you to sleep."

I shook my head at her. Having her the two times I did wasn't something I'd regret. "I'm okay. I'm not a hundred percent but I'm okay."

That was part truth. I was probably around sixty percent myself and would have preferred to be a hundred percent me for this venture into uncertainty. I trusted my body and wasn't used to this near useless version of me.

"I'm worried about you."

"Don't, I'm a lot better."

"Xander, I wished we could have taken you to a hospital. I would feel better if you had some kind of scan."

"There's no time for that. I'm gonna have to be as okay as I can be, but I promise I'll go as soon as I can."

"You'd better, I'm not going to go through so much to lose you to something I should have taken better heed of."

It was nice to have her care about me the way she did. I hadn't had that in a very long time.

"Are you okay with today?"

"I'm scared. I'm just sitting on edge waiting for something to happen. It's not nice to feel like that. I wish we had some idea of what's going on with my father. We don't though. He'll be looking for me, Xander. He has access to stuff. Things beyond my imagination."

That was what concerned me. "Don't worry. We just keep moving. Where we're going we should be safe." We would be. Jack was Jack but he had contacts too and I supposed I had Ethan. I definitely had Wes. I just needed to be on my turf. That was it, my turf. If something happened there then I knew I'd be able to handle it.

"Jack sounds nice."

I'd talked a little more about him last night. It was not only going to be strange to see him because according to him I was presumed dead and had died five years ago, but I was going to be bringing a woman to the house that I was interested in. To him that person for me had been his daughter, Claire.

It was going to be a very awkward reunion. One that had to take place though.

"He's nice."

She nodded. "Okay, let's... do this."

Let's do this.

I would have definitely felt better though if I'd had my full strength.

I planned it out well.

Frankie readied the truck and we left before four. It was good to get as far as we could under the darkness.

By five we were just going by Coyote Springs. The road had been clear and we covered a lot of miles in the space between, putting us ahead of the traffic.

Now it seemed like we were approaching it.

Frankie glanced at the rearview mirror but he wasn't looking at me, he was looking at something I couldn't see. Something on the road. Behind us.

"What's up?" I asked.

"Car and a bike. They been following us, I'm sure of it. Picked 'em up about half an hour ago. They followed even when I took the shortcut at Dry Lake," Frankie answered.

His eyes darted between the road ahead and the mirror.

Jia straightened up, worry instantly filled her face.

I looked behind me and gazed out the back window to try and find the car and bike.

"It's the black Kawasaki and the black Porsche," Frankie clarified.

I saw them. They were a few cars back. Just from looking I couldn't tell if they were actually following, but if Frankie thought they were then I wouldn't doubt him. He would have been paying more attention to something like that.

Jia looked too. "I can't tell if it's one of Pa's people," she stated.

I just couldn't tell.

"I'm gonna divert down Wells. There's no reason for them to turn off with us. If they do then I think it's safe to say we've been found." Frankie sped up a little more.

"What are we going to do?" Jia asked.

"We can't get the cops on our ass. That would not be good. I'd really hoped we wouldn't draw attention to ourselves. The number plates must have popped up on the radar."

"How far out will Wells put us?" I asked. I didn't know the roads here very well. Just the central routes I'd taken over the last month.

"Completely off, but it's that or stay on Route 93 for longer than we have to, and if they start shooting…" He quirked a brow.

That would not be good. It wasn't all that busy but it would get that way soon. Shooting meant civilians could get caught up and shit, it meant us being dead, dead, dead.

"Gotcha."

"There's a gun under your seat." Frankie glanced over his shoulder. I reached down and pulled out an impressive looking shotgun. I had to say that Frankie most assuredly didn't pack light. He'd packed the ammo that could get the job done with one hit.

"Got it," I told him, with a firm nod.

He nodded back then glanced at Jia. "Jia baby girl keep your head down. Please, and buckle up. This could get real nasty."

While Jia strapped herself in and tightened the belt to more than comfortable, Frankie sped up even more.

I looked behind us and damn it to fuck, the bike and car sped up too.

It was enough for me to agree on them following us for sure. The other surety was them turning too when we turned off the road to Wells.

"We definitely got company," I shouted.

Thank God the road ahead was clear. No after five traffic yet. This road looked like it was taking us back to desert land.

Jesus Christ I didn't know why I'd bothered to hope this part could run smoothly. Of course it wouldn't, it made me wonder about alternative routes, providing we made it out of this.

Fuck they were speeding up when we sped up and gaining on us. The bike was very close.

Frankie accelerated and pulled out a revolver from

his jacket pocket. Jia put her head down when she saw that and curled next to me. I hated putting her in danger.

Again.

The biker pulled a gun from his backpack and fired a shot. It hit the back of the car and jerked us.

That lanced me up for action. I'd get this mother-fucker before he got the chance to do that again. I got to my knees, lowered the window and became the dare-devil I was by sticking my head out.

Frankie was a real demon on the road and his brain seemed synced to mine. He swerved across the road to give me a direct line of passage with the biker who was getting ready to shoot our wheels off.

When he saw the shotgun aiming at him though he switched up, but not fast enough. One shot and I took him down. The bullet went straight to his head, blew him backwards off the bike and the bike and him went tumbling over the side of the road.

One down, one car to go and it didn't look like these guys in the car came to mess around.

I saw a machine gun and pulled my head back in just before they opened fire.

Fuck! They hit us. Jia screamed.

"Frankie try and drive faster if you can! Get as much space between us," I shouted.

QUEEN OF HIS HEART

Frankie did as I said putting his gun down so he could focus on driving.

That was best. He'd have to do that while I did the shooting.

More shots were fired and all I could do was hope the wheels stayed intact. Now was not a good time to lose our ride.

There was no good time to lose our ride.

I thought of a plan as I conjured up the image of the men in the car. I was pretty certain I'd seen three men. They'd looked like shadowy figures against the tinted windows and the bright morning sunlight.

On three I'd stick my head out again and aim for the driver. Hitting him would cause their car to swerve off-road and take them out.

One. Two. Three.

I bolted up again, stuck my head out and fired a shot. It echoed and got the car but fuck, it didn't get the driver. They were still coming for us, still driving to us.

The guy in the passenger seat put his head out again with the machine gun. I fired a shot and missed.

I went back inside the car and Frankie frowned.

"Hold tight guys, let's get down here. Thousand Spring Creek." He motioned to our left. There was a thicket of trees in a woodland area, it was perfect.

He bumbled down the road and sped off. Jia

83

screamed again, cowering against the noise, the gun shots, the panic and terror.

The car followed us and started firing shots again.

Jesus if we weren't careful this could really be it. It could be it.

Frankie sped to the trees and the path became rocky, jagged, bumpy.

Once again I thought of the driver of the Porsche. I had to get him.

On three, I moved and fired one shot, growling as I did so.

It got him.

It got them and the car jerked up on the path then smashed into a tree.

It didn't matter who else got taken out in the car, we lost them.

"You guys okay?" I asked both of them but I checked Jia.

She was shaking but she was okay.

"I'm fine."

I looked to Frankie and saw his arm was covered with blood. *Fuck*, he'd been hit.

"Frankie where'd they get you?"

"It's just my arm. We need to keep going."

"I'll drive," Jia offered. "Stop the truck. I'll drive."

"I should drive," I cut in.

She shook her head. "No, I can't do what you do and

I can't curl up and hide. I can help. Me on the wheel means you and Frankie can shoot if necessary. Frankie needs a bandage."

I liked her way of thinking. What I didn't like was the fact that if we had a repeat of just now she wouldn't be able to keep her head down.

She reached forward and touched my face. "I'll be okay. I will," she assured me.

I nodded and looked to Frankie. "Stop the truck Frankie and get back here."

He pulled the truck to a stop and he and Jia switched.

When she started driving down the path, I looked over Frankie's wound which looked bad. I grabbed one of the t-shirts his mother had given us and bandaged his arm with it, hoping the bleeding would stop.

"I'm good, kid. Don't worry about me. It just hurts like a son of a bitch." He chuckled. I'd only known a few people like him, who could take a bullet and act like it was a fucking scratch.

"You sure Frankie? We should get you to the hospital."

"Kid, we can't stop for that. This just got next level bad. We gotta lose the truck. Aside from my plates giving us away and acting like a homing beacon, we can't ride around all day with a bullet riddled truck. People will notice." He chuckled deep and hearty, as if he was fine. Although I could see he was in pain, just taking it really well. He was right though. We had to lose the truck.

"What do you have in mind?"

"I know a guy who can give us a ride. We just have to hope we don't have any more surprises along the way," he answered then looked to Jia. "Princess, switch the route on the GPS to Park Valley."

Jia did as he said.

We got to Park Valley two hours later and saw Frankie's contact.

I said a silent prayer of thanks that we didn't get any more surprises on the damn way. I didn't know if I could take it. The worry over Jia would get me and probably give me a heart attack.

We got into a Range Rover and I decided to take over driving.

With the new truck I had more assurance that we would be able to get to Idaho without any more hassle. Unless Giovanni had some wicked bad high tech satellite imaging recognition that could pick out our faces if we got caught driving by one of the cameras on the highway.

It was some sort of NASA tech I'd heard about and I

really hoped that was just my imagination running wild and not reality.

I could see it happening though. He was crazy enough and powerful enough to have that type of asset. Jia was what he wanted. His daughter.

The shootout earlier made me wonder though if he didn't care whether he got her back dead or alive. The men shooting weren't exactly careful, but then you couldn't really be careful in a scenario like that, you could only be as careful as you could be.

As soon as we left Park Valley we diverted towards Salt Lake City.

I thought it would be a good place to stop for a while. By the time we reached it, we'd already been on the road for ten hours with the delay in stopping over at Park Valley and of course the shootout. I'd been hoping that we would have gotten closer to our destination but it was okay.

While we were there we got some bandages for Frankie. I would have preferred to have gone to the walk-in medical center but it would be a little difficult to explain a bullet wound.

My plan was Jack. He'd be able to look at it.

We stopped in Salt Lake City for about six hours and we all just slept in the truck.

Frankie and I alternated between keeping watch for two hours each while the other got some sleep. We set off early morning again and headed to Boise, Idaho.

Just like in my younger days, the air was the first thing I noticed to change. It was fresh and had that mountain spring cleanliness to it.

That was the first thing that I'd noticed when Jack brought me here to live. Living in Chicago for most of my life I tended to notice things like that. City to Country.

Jack was originally from Montana; his family had a farm there so he knew exactly what I meant when I'd commented on it, he really did. I thought at the time that he appreciated that I noticed.

It was here that I'd decided I wanted to become a marine and go on some of the types of adventures he went on.

As I drove over the State line and saw the Welcome to Idaho sign, memories came flooding back into my mind.

All of it from start to finish. Or rather where I'd decided it should end.

I could have come back before now. I should have. It would have been right. I just couldn't face Jack. I promised I'd take care of Claire and I wasn't able to stop her from dying.

From being killed.

I felt like a failure and a failure of the worst kind.

The kind that was seeking justice and hadn't found it. Five long years and I hadn't been able to bring Balthazar down to his knees and chop off his damn head for what he'd done.

Jia reached across and tapped my hand, pulling me out of my thoughts.

I'd almost forgotten she was next to me. Frankie was in the back watching the scenery change as we rode by.

"You okay?" she asked. "You look worried."

"I am."

She knew why I'd be worried. "Don't be, I think he'll be more than happy to see you."

"I really hope so."

I was about to find out.

I turned down North Cartwright Road that led to Hidden Springs. Jack lived off there in a plantation style house.

Two minutes down the road and I could see it.

It was five thirty. The sun was bright already but still held that subtle presence of peeking through to start the new day.

If I knew Jack, he would be up already tending to the horses.

The house I'd loved so much came into view and I turned down the long drive, passing the fields and the lake.

I'd forgotten how big the place was, it was huge.

I pulled up just outside the house across from his truck. He had that same beat up pickup he called Bertha.

God, I'd missed him. He was Claire's father but he'd felt like mine too.

The door to the stables opened and my heart stilled when Jack stepped out. His face contorted with curiosity as to who would be coming to his home at this hour.

He took off his heavy duty work gloves and started walking toward us.

When I opened the door and stepped out he stopped short and stared on ahead at me, his lips parted and shock registered on his face.

Jack looked the same, a little older but roughly the same. Most guys who were ex-military tended to take care of themselves. Jack was no exception. He still looked tough like he could kill you. A little like a cross between Bruce Willis and Hugh Jackman. That was what Jack looked like.

I froze, not knowing what him stopping meant.

Did he stop because anger made him stop, or did he stop because of the surprise.

I didn't know and the not knowing seized me up, preventing me from moving forward.

Hope however filled my heart when he took a step toward me.

Hope I hadn't realized I'd wanted badly, and for years.

One more step, then another and I started walking to him too.

We met each other halfway and he looked me over with that classic look. Like he'd just seen a ghost.

He wasn't far off since I'd been a ghost for the last five years.

"Xander? Is that really you?" he asked. His voice was heavy with emotion.

When I nodded a tear ran down his cheek and he pulled me in for a hug.

CHAPTER 8

Xander

It was so strange being back.

Being home.

Home.

Over the last few years I'd had some days where it felt like I'd never return. When I thought about it now, it was clear to me that I'd been on a mission of vengeance that would have carried me to the last days of my life.

Looking for Balthazar Kane and trying to find answers was like digging around a haystack looking for that proverbial needle. It was people like him who gave weight to sayings like that.

Simply because it was difficult.

Difficult but not impossible, but bordering near enough on the impossible.

Seeing Jack now made me see that realistically I'd erred on the side of failure because I couldn't face him.

After that very emotion-filled reunion that saw me in tears too, we went inside the house. There the bulk of the time was spent tending to Frankie.

Just as I'd thought, Jack knew exactly what to do. The man was medically trained and just the sort of person we needed, who understood why we couldn't pitch up to the hospital without answering some very important questions that would undoubtedly land us in trouble. More shit.

Jack skillfully removed the bullet from Frankie's arm, patched him back up, and set him up in a room the way Frankie set me up at his family's home.

Once we were all packed out with the little we had, I joined Jack for the looming conversation we needed to have.

The conversation that was a combo of two very big matters. The most pressing questions were where I'd been for the last five years and what happened to me. I'd practically returned from the dead.

The next big conversation was Giovanni, Jia and Frankie.

I'd pitched up on Jack's drive in trouble, just like when I first met him at sixteen years old.

I couldn't believe that was twenty years ago.

Twenty years ago I snuck into his garage, injured from being beaten up after a job with mobsters went wrong. I'd thought then that I was in the deepest shit of my life. It was my first taste of mafia guys and the last until this recent stint with Giovanni. It was enough however to teach me a damn good lesson.

Twenty years later I was in trouble again. Worse than ever before.

We sat in the kitchen at the breakfast table, opposite each other. It was close to lunchtime and the sun beamed through the window in all its glory.

It seemed brighter to me here, like everything felt more enhanced.

The thought was stupid because like the moon, the sun was the same. Couldn't really vary in brightness across the states. Maybe across the world in some parts but not the way I was thinking.

"I kept imagining this," Jack stated. He ran a hand through his salt and pepper hair and gazed across at me with that fatherly warmth I'd always appreciated.

I looked back to him. "That I'd come to you clearly in trouble again?" I might have been going for some element of humor but didn't manage to pull it off. There was nothing funny or humorous in any of this situation.

He gave me a warm smile and rested his elbows on the table.

"Xander, this is me. I've waited years for this and I want you to be real with me. That was the first thing I asked you when we first met. Remember?"

"I remember Sir. Back then I had fewer secrets."

"It's not about the amount of secrets you have, son. It's the content that defines them. Now I'm sitting here looking at a man who I consider my son. I was told he was dead, I even got his dog tags. I buried you, or what they told me was left of you and still I refused to believe it was true."

His gaze clung to mine and I couldn't look away.

"You didn't believe it?"

He shook his head. "I didn't believe it. *Claire...* she was a different story. I knew in my heart from the minute that girl decided she wanted to follow in her old man's shoes that I was going to get that call one day. The call telling me something had happened to her. I knew it. I did. Just like me, she did plenty of things that were reckless. Unlike me though, she didn't have that stroke of luck. For me I got lucky one last time and I threw in the towel. I saw it for what it was and took hold of the chance it gave me. I suspect Claire wouldn't have done that. She would have kept on going until it killed her. She got that part from her mother." He nodded.

His words tugged heavily on my heart. They were true.

I felt they were true and that part wasn't me looking for an excuse so I wouldn't blame myself.

Claire was a mixture of her fearless father, and her daunting mother who knew giving birth to her child could kill her but she did it anyway. That was how her mother died. In childbirth.

Just like mine. My mother died during child birth too and we always talked about that element of similarity we had. I knew for damn certain that I got my guts and courage from my mother.

I'd always considered that when I was with Claire. I imagined her mother making it her mission to give birth to her baby and sacrifice herself if she needed to. Her life a price to pay for what she wanted most.

That was what Claire was like and she would have indeed kept going until something stopped her. There were many times we got lucky, she just kept going though.

"I told you I'd take care of her." My gaze dropped to the table and I sighed. When I looked back to him there was nothing but understanding in his eyes.

"And that was nice of you, but there would have

only been so much of that you could do. She was her own person. Strong-willed and strong minded. So much more than me. But, I felt it in my bones that something would happen. It was almost a damn given and I prepared for it for years. I was told it was a bomb that took out the team in Nepal. They brought me her tags and yours."

He paused and silence filled the space between us, opening the floor for me to speak.

As the conversation had taken the direction of the past first, I thought that was where I needed to start. I'd start at the past and work my way forward.

"It wasn't just a bomb. That came after." That was the best way I could start. Everything I would tell him next was top secret. This man however, was a man I had no secrets from. He was ex- military, ex-CIA, ex-SMF. We knew when to talk and when not to. He knew when I could and should talk and right now I owed no allegiance to anyone.

I drew in a breath and continued my recount. "We'd been tracking a man called Balthazar Kane for years. Approximately three. The situation with him had gotten so bad, we were ring fenced to deal with every-thing to do with him. *Everything*."

I told him everything from the past and finished with Claire's death and what should have been mine too.

That was the end of that saga.

He gazed down at the table as he processed the information. It was a lot. Fucking a lot to tell and a lot to take on board.

"I've spent the last five years trying to find Balthazar," I added. "Never getting close. I went off on my own mission trying to find the son of a bitch and never once got near enough until days ago."

Jack lifted his head. "*Days*, son?"

"Yeah that brings me to the next part of the story. Weeks ago I was commissioned by Ethan to do a job. He found me. The man found me. Following the success of the mission the promise was to assist me to find Balthazar Kane. It was the only reason I agreed to it. The job was to steal back some blueprints from a mob boss. The blueprints were for a super nuke. I never realized the job would include a web of several layers of traps and players like you wouldn't believe."

By the time I finished telling him everything Jack was completely blown away. I could see the intrigue in his eyes and the expression on his face. Hearing the details of the past was a lot to take in, but the more recent stuff was like I was talking about some Hollywood Michael Bay film, minus the blowing up of buildings. That was what it felt like, living in a film like that.

"Fucking hell, Xander. What the actual hell?" He

shook his head. "All of that? And Balthazar Kane in the mix?"

"Yes. So I'm here. It sent me here to you. I didn't want to involve you. I never did before because you're my family. You are, and I wanted to keep you out of it. I stayed dead because I thought it would give me some advantage to find Balthazar. He thought he killed me so I became the shadow and hoped it would end somewhere. Then this all happened."

"You are very lucky Xander. Very lucky."

"I owe my luck to Frankie. He didn't have to help me."

"No he didn't."

"I know he's got to be worried about his family." I would be if I were him. He'd said Giovanni wouldn't come for his family but I wouldn't put it past him to try. It was natural for me to factor that in.

"Of course. And um… the girl?"

My breath stilled. I'll admit I avoided talking too much about Jia. I shouldn't though. I was serious about her and I meant what I said when I asked her to be mine.

I wanted her to be mine in every essence of the word. I wanted her to be mine and when that day came I was done doing all of this.

I was completely done. I'd go to Europe with her

and she could do what she wanted. There were many things I was good at so I wasn't worried about myself.

When I asked her to be mine, I felt it was right to ask, so she would know I wasn't just with her for now.

Talking to Jack about her though would be difficult. The only woman I'd ever spoken to him about was his daughter.

"I'm not going to let her father get her Jack," I declared.

He nodded. "Because you love her."

It wasn't a question. It was a statement.

I nodded but I knew the awkwardness of the affirmation was evident.

I hung my head down feeling the weight of it, feeling a little more of that failure of being unable to take care of his daughter like I said I would.

Then he reached across the table and tapped my knuckles.

I looked up, met his gaze and pressed my lips together.

"Xander, you don't have to feel bad admitting your love for someone else. It's been five years since Claire. I would have hoped you'd move on. She would have definitely wanted you to."

"It's hard. It was hard. I will never stop loving Claire, Jack. I never forgot her."

He gave me a curt nod accompanied by a warm

QUEEN OF HIS HEART

smile. "I know, that's something I know and you don't have to explain anything to me when it comes to that. Way back when, there would have been very few people I would have allowed to date my girl. I could see your love for her from day one. It was never a question to me or a wonder. And I know it wasn't the kind you forget."

"Thanks, that means a lot."

"Good. By the same token I know this girl, this woman –Jia Marchesi –must mean a lot to you to put your neck on the line with the mob."

Jesus, when he said it like that I definitely felt the gravity of the situation weighing down on my shoulders.

"What the hell am I gonna do Jack? It's all so complicated."

"One step at a time boy. What have I always told you about complicated?"

I smiled. "Complicated is a bullshit word to cloud over something that *looks* difficult."

He chuckled and nodded. "And what have I always said about difficult?"

"Go back to the place where it all began, the part where it was easy. Start from there and work my way forwards."

He made a show of clapping. "Well done my boy. So let's do this. Start where it all began."

I thought for a moment and decided to retrace the

events that had occurred. "Giovanni steals the blue-prints and becomes a threat to national security. The Ra try to steal them from him but are unsuccessful. He gets away and hides the prints then I get hired to steal them back." That was the first part.

That was exactly what happened at the beginning.

Jack narrowed his eyes though. "There are missing parts to that story."

"What do you mean?" I wasn't following what he meant. That was what happened.

"It doesn't fit. Giovanni is small time and The Chameleon does not work like that. Not so messy so that the Ra would simply find out. They would have been told, the question is by who."

Shock seized my next breath. Giovanni had said the same thing. So did Frankie. Jack saying it too was abso-lutely something to take note of. It carried all the weight of significance it could have for a man like him to point that out. I hadn't even thought of it myself. Me with all my exposure to The Ra and Balthazar.

"There's a rat in Giovanni's circle," I informed him. I was sure now from what Frankie had said that the rat had to be Armand. It made sense and fit.

"The rat is just a rat, an enabler. Less than small time. There's no way that guy would have been able to make contact with the Ra much less be in touch with a man like Balthazar."

QUEEN OF HIS HEART

"Damn it to hell. Who could it be?"

"My guess is since the blueprints are what I would a hundred percent label as classified, the only people who could have known they were stolen would have come from high up. Like CIA or SMF high up." He held my gaze and my attention. "If someone high up knew about the prints being stolen then only they could have passed on the intel to Balthazar. No mere rat could have done that. The rat's just part of the game."

My blood ran cold. It ran cold and my thoughts stilled. "You think someone in the CIA or SMF is working with the Ra?"

He raised his shoulders into a shrug. "Xander I think you're aware that I trust no one and the most valuable lesson I could have taught you is that everyone has a price. Everybody can be bought. If you fall outside that category then that's great but it's something you have to bear in mind."

"Ethan said the SMF had been called in to deal with the situation."

"Maybe because it got out of hand. That's usually when you guys get called in, right? So they needed you." He nodded.

I wasn't sure what the hell to do now.

Don't trust anybody?

Right.

Earlier I'd messaged Wes to let him know where I

was. He said Ethan was still with him working on stuff in Vegas, but he'd come. He was on the way here.

I'd thought at the time that I would speak to Ethan separately. Now it was looking like I needed to. Someone was using him, had used him and I had to find some way of stopping him from getting the prints, and getting the prints back to headquarters.

"There's a guy I know, a contact of mine with skills a little like yours. Can hack most systems without leaving a trace. He's good with backtracking. Very old school. I reckon your skills combined could give you more answers," Jack suggested.

Answers would be good.

It was what I needed to get me on track. Some answers would give direction.

"I need to meet with him soon as."

Jack nodded. "I'll set something up for tomorrow."

"Thanks Jack. I'm grateful."

My nerves spiked with a sense of awareness. The CIA or SMF working with Balthazar and The Ra.

Shit!

That was definitely something new and an angle I'd never explored before.

It wasn't something I would have even thought of because it was so damn bizarre.

CHAPTER 9

Jia

I WOULDN'T DENY that it felt a little strange being here.

Jack was really nice.

The kind of nice I would have loved from my own father. To me he was the opposite of Pa.

Or maybe a different version of what Pa could have been like. Tough and in his late fifties with muscle that showed his years of looking after himself to get that way, and what he'd done for work.

That was what Pa was like and Jack seemed the same. Except my father was evil. Jack was not.

And...

Jack had a daughter who loved Xander and Xander loved her so much he wanted to spend forever with her.

Was it wrong to be jealous of a perfect woman who was dead? Especially when just the other night Xander asked me to be his.

Was I crazy?

Maybe it was just being here.

We'd been here all day and it was the first time I'd felt safe since leaving the airport. It was the first time.

It was the first moment when I could actually stop and take a breath but I wasn't sure if I could, so it was just after two in the morning and I was sitting by the window with two great views to capture my heart.

The first view was of my man sleeping in the king-size bed in the center of the room. We didn't have to be quiet here earlier when we had sex and I made him think I was going to drift off to sleep in his arms.

This room was on the other side of the house in what I thought classed as a wing. Or at the very least an apartment style setting fit for a couple. This was Xander's old room. He'd told me when he'd first moved here Jack had set it up so it was like he could have his own privacy and space.

I came from wealth so I knew what space was. This was definitely comparable to that, just cleaner.

Cleaner like the view before me of the landscape.

I loved it from the second we'd entered Idaho. I'd

never been here before but it was just the place where an artist like me could fall in love with the landscape. Definitely fall in love.

I fell and now I was taking every opportunity I could get.

The thing I thought of first was that painting I'd promised Xander. I didn't have my paints or anything but what I did have was a good old number two pencil and a large notepad I'd found earlier. Jack gave it to me when he saw me looking at it. I'd told him I was an artist.

Since I couldn't sleep and it didn't look like I was going to bed any time soon, I wanted to make use of the time.

I drew Xander standing by the lake.

All from my imagination and what I'd conjured up even though I was staring out at the lake now and it couldn't have been darker outside. I'd drawn the parts illuminated by the moon.

That was it, just those parts and I imagined what they must have been like in the sunlight with Xander standing next to them.

I gave him a half smile. He never fully smiled at anything except for when he was flirting or being charming, or cocky. Or when I took my clothes off.

Most of the time it was a half-smile, almost like he was showing that he took note of something to smile at, but holding off to maintain that cool edge.

I looked over to him and watched him sleep. Deep in slumber he was, looking like he needed it. I supposed we all did really and I should be sleeping too.

I returned my gaze to the shadows of night outside the window and the smooth breath of wind that rippled over the lake. It made me think of Pa, what he must have been doing now.

I could almost feel his worry. Worry over me.

No, not almost. I could feel it, no matter how far we were I could feel it.

This would have been the first time in my life that I'd done this, and realistically this was the very thing that I'd thought of doing weeks ago. Escaping.

I'd wanted to escape his controlling hand.

My sketchy plan had been to take small amounts of cash every other day in a week from my account so he wouldn't notice. Then I'd make a move and run off. Pa was clever though. He stopped me right in my damn tracks with that plan. It was at that point too, that I realized just how bad things were. That something else, or rather something more than usual was going on.

That something led me here.

Here as in right now, as I wondered if it was fair to allow not just Xander but Frankie to be part of this fiasco. The crux of the matter was we were now running from my father. Because of me.

If Pa found us he wouldn't hesitate to kill Xander and Frankie.

Death.

It would always come back to that, somewhere in the mix it would come back to that.

Death and dying. Was it fair to be selfish with the man I loved when realistically this probably would never be over?

That was why I was jealous of Claire. She didn't come from a bad seed. She didn't come from bad. Everything here was goodness. Everything in pureness.

Xander shuffled in the bed. I turned to look at him and smiled when his hands reached over to the space where I'd laid beside him.

"Baby…" He breathed and shuffled to sit up.

He looked straight at me. The moonlight lit him up and just like the other night, he looked perfect.

He slipped off the bed showing off that body of his. In his Calvin Klein's, that walking advert came to my mind again.

"Jia what are you doing? You should…" His voice trailed off when he saw my drawing. He looked at me and smiled, then pulled up the other chair to sit in front of me.

I handed him the sketch pad when he reached for it.

"Jia, this is amazing. I'm always blown away by your talent."

"Thank you. I'm glad you like it because it's yours."

He raised his brows and smiled wide.

An unexpected smile. I forgot and now thought I had to give more credit to his smile where it was due... he smiled like that when he was with me.

Yes... that was more accurate. He smiled showing me his soul when he was with me.

"My damn, Jia you never cease to amaze me. I love it."

"It's not quite finished yet."

"What more could you do to it?" He looked intrigued to know.

"It's just little finishing touches. Like here." I pointed at the drawing and hovered over the right side of his face there. "You have a dimple. It comes out when you're smiling like that. Just that one though. The left comes out when you smile wider then it reaches your eyes."

Now he looked fascinated. "You memorized all that about me?"

"I did. So I want it to look perfect." *Just in case...*

It was a dark afterthought. Just in case something happened and this was all he had to remember me by, or just in case the worst happened to all of us.

He set the sketchpad down and took my hands into his.

"What's up? The drawing is amazing but I know you

wouldn't just be here sitting by the window drawing me at two in the morning. It's maybe a stupid question to ask but I'm asking. I want you to talk to me."

"It's everything Xander."

"Want to start with one of those things?"

Like the comparisons I'd been making between myself and Claire? I probably shouldn't start with that.

"It's understandable if you feel strange being here. I mean in Jack's house, and he was Claire's father."

He'd read my mind.

I pulled in a breath. "Am I that transparent?" I gave him a hopeless smile.

"Not so much, but I imagined you might feel like that. I kind of did earlier, so it's understandable. It's natural."

"I think part of me wonders –dare I hope we pull through this –how I'll fair in comparison to someone you loved practically your whole life. It was long enough right? Long enough to be classed as a lifetime. We haven't known each other like that. I know I love you, but I can't be like her. My father is a mob boss and hers is this awesome person. I'm just –" He stopped my next words with a kiss.

It was a kiss to seal all. The kind that set the tone for what we did next. He reached forward and smoothed his hands behind my head, angling my face so he could deepen the kiss.

I cupped his face and moved closer to him, pressing against him. I was wearing a t-shirt. It was one of his old ones so it caught me at the edge of my hips and looked more like a night shirt.

When that came off I knew we'd be heading straight back to the bed.

No more words needed to be spoken.

I understood that he was showing me how he felt and I allowed him to.

He picked me up and carried me over to the bed, setting me down on my back then sliding off my panties.

Instead of the usual teasings and insane foreplay, he touched me differently.

More sensual, more purposeful.

He lowered to the valley between my breasts and kissed his way across to each nipple to suck just hard enough and long enough to make me wet, then he kissed his way down to my mound and kissed around my entrance, licking and stroking. It was just enough to turn me on.

The rest would come after.

He shrugged out of his boxers and came back to me, lifting my leg up and hooking it over his shoulder. Then he guided the fat head of his cock straight into my pussy, plunging in deep.

I gasped into the overwhelming pleasure and luxuriated in the sensation of his purposefully slow pumps which were a slow grind into my body, slow and sure then a little faster.

I grabbed against the cotton sheets as the moans fell from my lips. Every time we did this it felt different. It felt better and better, mind-blowing and mind-numbing in every way.

He sped up but going at a rhythm we both enjoyed and got lost in.

"Xander..." I groaned. It reached a point where it felt too good.

It was so damn good I started grinding against his ruthless cock pounding into me. That made him pound harder and jackhammer at the pace he would usually in the wild reckless manner that consumed me and severed my brain from reality.

Fuck, I was coming. I was ... near.

No... *there.*

I arched into the bed and cried out my release. Fire licking over my skin like shards of electricity.

"Good girl, scream if you want to."

I obeyed, screaming.

He caught my hand and lowered so that his face was eye level with mine and he started rutting into me at a speed that made the tension coil in my groin again.

The speed curated another orgasm comparable to

the stuff I'd only ever read about or dreamt up in a fantasy.

The man consumed me, sending me over the edge once more but this time he came too, pounding in me with his relentless thrusts then thundering his hot cum inside me. I savored the feel of it burning up the walls of my core.

We stayed just like that for a few minutes, breathing hard, hearts pounding, my ears drumming from the wildness.

It was amazing how sleep hadn't come for me before but suddenly I was exhausted.

Xander moved up to be closer to me then cupped my face and gazed deeply into my eyes.

"Doesn't matter how long," he stated.

I had to think hard about what he was talking about but then I remembered. I'd mentioned that he hadn't known me long.

"Do you want to be with me Jia?" he asked. I had to wonder if that was a trick question or a rhetorical one.

"You know I do."

"Say it."

I touched his face. "I want to be with you."

"That's all I need. All I need to know, it's all that matters to me, and time is irrelevant. It's just a thing. You can't compare yourself to anybody, no matter who they are or what they meant to me. There's only one of you Jia. Just one and I want to be with you too."

"Thank you." I'd never felt more valued in my life. "But Xander, how could I claim to love you and put you through this? Running from my father. It will get to a point where it won't just be him."

"I know Jia. I've factored that in, but I won't let him take you. He'll have to kill me first."

That was supposed to show me the depth of his seriousness, but it was the very thing I was worried about.

Him dying.

For me...

CHAPTER 10

Xander

I WATCHED JIA GET READY, looking like she was doing her best to stave off the worry. She always had that uneasy look when she was worried. It would dim her bright blue gaze.

"Does it look good on me?" She asked giving me a little twirl.

She was wearing one of Claire's summer dresses. She looked amazing.

"You look perfect."

"Really?"

"Hmmm hmmm."

We'd come in here to look for some clothes. We both felt awkward doing so but it was stupid to have a room full of women's wear and have her in my shirts.

I'd sat on the edge of the bed watching her, focusing on her and not thinking about where I was. Claire's room.

Jack had kept it the same. The exact same.

Same as when we'd gone to college and practically moved out, both our rooms were intact.

I pushed the thought out of my head and gave my undivided to the beautiful woman in front of me. It was better not to think of the past. Less painful.

"You're just saying that. These clothes are tiny. I barely fit." She pretended to pout.

The only reason she barely fit was because of those double D's. It was a reason most women would kill for. There was no complaint needed at all.

"Baby, the only thing that looks better on you is nothing." That was truth, only her naked body could rival how she looked now.

She widened her eyes and glanced over her shoulder.

"Xander," she chided and swat my hands away when I tried to touch her breasts. "Jack's down the hall."

"He didn't hear me, and he won't see me either," I teased.

She rolled her eyes at me. "What am I going to do with you?"

I reached for her tiny waist and pulled her to me. "Woman you know exactly what to do with me." I was trying for lighthearted to cheer her up.

"I do." She leaned closer to my ear and giggled in that sexy way that I loved. "I plan to do a lot with you when you get back. Including that thing you really like."

Now it was my turn to widen my eyes since I loved everything she did to me. She could do it all.

"I need to hurry back then."

"Yes I agree, you definitely need to hurry back."

I drew her down for a kiss.

I was going to see Jack's contact. His name was Dorian Patterson. He was an ex-military man who worked the cyber terrorism division as an senior intelligence analyst. The minute I heard that I thought he sounded right up my alley. I hadn't had the privilege of doing much hacking in this gig, so this would be cool. It put my computer science skills to good use.

The worry returned to her eyes when she moved away from me.

"How long will you be gone for?" she asked.

"Not sure baby, I'm not really sure what we'll be doing." The only good thing was that Wes would be joining me there.

Frankie was going to stay here with Jia and Jack.

Depending on what I found, that would be when I contacted Ethan. It wouldn't help me much with everything else but I guess I was considering it as my last attempt to help, since I blew the mission by getting caught.

Part of me was hoping for some help with keeping Giovanni off my back too.

I wasn't, however, relying on it though. It wasn't their problem or their worry that I'd taken the man's daughter and declared her mine.

"Then what Xander? I don't think we can stay here forever."

"Brazil." That was what came to me last night. We needed to sort some stuff though.

She smiled at that. "Really? Brazil?"

"Yeah, for a little while, just till it blows over, then Europe."

I actually saw the hope fill her eyes and a sheen of light fill them.

"Europe? You'd want to go there with me?"

I nodded. "Yeah. We can find somewhere in Europe."

"Not Italy, that will be worse."

I chuckled. "I imagine so."

"Spain is nice." She smiled and leaned down to kiss me again. "Thank you Xander. I love that you thought of me in such a way. We don't have to go to Europe though. We could just go somewhere we'll both be happy. I want you to be able to do what you want too."

"We'll talk and see where's best. Try not to worry about what's happening. You'll be okay with Jack and Frankie while I'm gone."

She beamed. "Jack's going to show me how to make blueberry muffins."

I laughed at that. "You'll love those. His taste like heaven if heaven had a taste."

"It's nice. I really love cooking. My mother made sure I could cook, but she wanted me to love it. Food tastes so much better when made with love."

"I believe you."

I stood up and took her hand. We walked out of the room and I closed the door, sealing away Claire's room. I'd probably never go back in there.

"I'll come say goodbye, just gonna see Frankie first."

She bobbed her head and gave me one last kiss before going down the stairs.

I made my way over to Frankie's room, he was just changing his dressing and looked stronger than he had when we arrived.

He acknowledged me as I came in with a nod. He was worried too.

"Hey pal everything good to go?" He asked. We'd spoken briefly earlier about what I was doing today.

"Yeah it's all good. It should be. Are you okay to stay here?"

"I'm fine. Don't worry about me. I'm thinking of where we can head to next. This place is a given Xander. Giovanni can find us here. It's where you *lived*. Can't stay here forever."

I agreed. "I know but we'll have more muscle here for a little while. I'm gonna see what I can do when I get back. Have you been in touch with your family?"

"Yeah, they're okay. No sign of trouble. Vinny's looking in on them for me and treading carefully."

That was good to hear.

"I'll do my best to get back here soon and we can come up with something solid," I promised.

"Cool."

He still looked tense but that was to be expected.

I left him hoping we could come up with something more today.

Wes hugged me hard when he saw me.

We met outside Dorian's house which was just a fraction smaller than Jack's place. He had the same sort of set up, with the land and lake and the house that looked like he'd had it custom built. It was nice with that homely feel.

I hugged Wes back, getting that emotional reunion feel again. Like we were brothers. When he pulled away he punched me hard in my arm.

"You fucking prick!" He scowled. "Don't you ever do that to me again. No more ass backwards plans where you get caught."

I held my hands up. "I know and I'm sorry."

"You aren't sorry, you'd fucking do it all over again."

I more than likely would. "Wes, come on man. You know I didn't have much choice. It was a shot I took. It blew up in my face but I had to take the chance."

"I know, but it was still fucked up. Ethan was freaking."

"What is he doing now?"

"He went back to liaise with his people. I think he was just happy you were alive. He did lose his shit though when we realized you'd been captured and I told him what happened."

"I know he must have."

"Didn't get to speak to your girl. I tried to call her a few times." He looked defeated. "But... prior to your message the other day, intel spied on Giovanni and listened in on a conversation with Armand. We heard Jia was missing. Also that Frankie took her, and helped you escape. We did the math and assumed she was with you." He raised his brows.

"Yeah. Lots has happened. I'll fill you in later. "

"Later? Come on Xander. I've been worried sick."

I could imagine that being true. "This first." I pointed to the house.

He looked over. "Well, what's this about?"

I thought it was best to wait until he got here to talk to him about why we were meeting Dorian.

"I just need some answers. This guy can do some backtracking. Jack thinks something was off in the beginning. He thinks The Ra got involved via someone higher. Like from the CIA or SMF."

Shock filled his face and his mouth dropped. "What the fuck?"

"Yeah I know, it makes sense. That's why I'm here. I just figured since I was unsuccessful I could still help in some way. I figured if he's right then that would be really bad."

"Fuck, of course. It would mean Ethan got hired and got used as a chump. All of us." He brought his hand to his head.

"Yes. All of us," I agreed trying to tamp down the anger that stirred at the thought.

"Well let's do this." Wes grit his teeth.

We walked up to the door and rang the bell. A thin wiry-looking man with red hair opened the door. He wore thick rimmed glasses that made his eyes look bigger.

"Hello." He beamed. I detected a hint of a Scottish

accent. "I suppose you're Xander and … Xander's friend?" Yup I was right, he had a Scottish accent.

He looked from me to Wes and smiled.

I put out my hand to shake his.

"Yes. I'm Xander and this is my friend Wes. Great to meet you."

"Same here."

Wes shook his hand too.

We walked inside the house and it was clear that the classic homely look stopped at the door.

The house reminded me of being in The Pentagon but with a mixture of what Tony Stark's place would look like, very, very high tech.

That was just the sitting room.

He led us to his office and it looked like it had been pulled from a scene in Iron Man. He even had robots.

"Jesus, what a place you have here," I stated.

"It's totally my kind of place," Wes agreed with keen appreciation.

Dorian smiled. "Glad you like it guys. This is what you call years of design."

I smiled at that. I could just imagine the years he must have put in.

Dorian took us over to a seated area. The computer was holographic and moved on a glass screen at the touch of his fingers.

"So, what can I do for you? Who are we spying on?" he asked.

I glanced at Wes then looked back to him.

"I'm not sure."

"This isn't gonna be one of those things where you can't tell me what I'm looking for because of some breach of protocol or shite like that, are ya?"

"No."

"Good, because I exist now outside of the system. I get the juice on things if the price is right. But some things I do for free. Like for friends like Jack. So this is a freebie."

"Thank you. We're looking for intel on the Ra. I think I want to see if we can find anything from somewhere, or someone in the CIA office or SMF that looks off. Maybe an email."

He inclined his head to the side. "I get it. That's deep shit though. You think there's a double agent amongst them?"

"Possibly. The correspondence would have gone out around seven or eight weeks ago. The name that should pop up is Giovanni Marchesi. And blue prints. Some blueprints containing nuke designs were stolen from an envoy in transit to Arizona."

"Okay. Let me see what I can find."

He tapped a few keys, his hands moving so fast I couldn't tell what he was writing out.

He tapped away and the screen populated with a lot of code. It was just programs he was hacking. Then I realized he was looking through a trail in the liquid file links.

It was a good thing Wes and I understood what he was doing because he wasn't one to explain as he went along.

"I'm not seeing anything that stands out on email. I'm gonna search on the phones linked to people in charge. Maybe I can pick up a text or something."

I raised my brows. "You can do that?" I hadn't done that before. Didn't have to. I'd mostly hacked government systems for information they were hiding.

"Oh yes. I can totally do that. I have this set up wired to give me all the juice. There is no tea spilling anywhere that I can't find. The hard part is the search. If we had a name it would help." He inclined his head to the side.

I was still impressed. It made me wonder what he'd done in his line of work.

"There's shit loads of info here." Wes stated.

There was a shit load. It was files Dorian searched with the reference blueprints. That was just the last few weeks.

"Dorian, how about localizing to one department at a time. SMF is smaller. How about focusing on the senior team maybe." There were five senior members of management.

Dorian looked more curious. "Got your focus on someone in particular?"

"Nah just trying to narrow the search. I was thinking that the information about the prints would have cascaded from the CIA. There may be something you can pick up there."

"Good thinking." He nodded.

"There'd be a lot of messages with the word 'prints' bouncing from Ethan however. Some to me, some to Wes. So don't focus on him."

Now he narrowed his eyes. "Xander, I leave no stone unturned. That's just me. I don't pussyfoot around shite or rule people out, it's why I'm so good."

"I get that but Ethan is clean." There was no part of it that fit him.

Wes brushed my elbow. "Xander there's no harm checking. Then we can rule him out."

"Sure, of course." It was true we could rule him out, even though I already had. Ethan had wanted to catch Balthazar as badly as me. In the past his orders were always to kill him on sight. No questions asked, just kill him if you got a clear shot.

Dorian scanned over the five members of the senior team. He brought up their files and the numbers associated with them that were listed. Each number was color coded.

"Right... so the red numbers are what we have on file for their business phones and personal phones. The yellow ones and blue are where my equipment goes a little further. Right now its tracked a cellphone number that has been used by each person over the last eight weeks," Dorian explained.

I looked at each person. Of the five people there. Ethan and Gina Hawkes had the most yellow codes, but they were the only ones with blue codes.

"What does yellow and blue specifically mean?" Wes asked. He took the words out of my mouth. I really hoped Dorian wasn't one of those people who just color coded all manner of unnecessary shit.

"Yellow is another personal number. I don't usually flicker an eyelid at that because of privacy. We may have their listed personal phone numbers but they may give their spouse, partners, kids, or other family members another number. It's common. I personally don't see the fun in having so many numbers but each to their own. The blue numbers are my pool of curiosity."

Okay, so it seemed like he wasn't one of those people who color coded for nothing.

He pulled in a breath and continued.

"This is where it gets highly illegal boys. Do I care? I

think not. It's the reason why you're here." He laughed. Wes cast a curious glance at me. "Blue usually means the phone was only used a couple of times and disposed of."

"I used a phone the other day that I had to get rid of," I surmised.

"Why'd you do that?" He raised a finger.

"So I couldn't be tracked."

He grinned. "Yes Xander, get with the program." He pointed back to the screen. "Let's start with her, she just has one blue code."

He tapped the number and it brought up a listing of all the text messages that had been sent to and received by the number. It also brought up a list of numbers which was a total number. Dorian tapped into the messages so we could look at each one. The first one was a dead giveaway that Mrs. Gina Hawkes was having an affair with the guy with the number ending 5567.

It said:

Don't worry my husband won't find out.
Come over in ten minutes and bring a pack of condoms.
We used the last one yesterday.

Dorian laughed and flicked through the rest of the messages which went from mild to super raunchy until the last message, when she told Mr. 5567 she couldn't see him anymore but it was fun.

"So, I'm gonna rule her out." Dorian bit the inside of his lip.

I agreed. Wes started laughing.

"I'd have a field day with a set up like this," Wes stated.

I shook my head at him, but the seriousness returned to me when Dorian switched the screen back to Ethan.

Ethan's picture came up first, then the number listing. I recognized one of the numbers in yellow. That was the number I corresponded with him on. Up to the other day that was the number I'd sent the code red to.

Dorian went to the first blue number.

"This one is the oldest. I'll start with that, it's dated back eight weeks," Dorian said, tapping into the number. Like on Gina's profile, the number came up with messages.

I'd already decided in my mind that the only thing these messages would contain in relation to Ethan was mission guidelines.

Until I saw the first message from Ethan.

Giovanni Marchesi has the blueprints. If we get our hands on those it's world domination. We can sell it to the highest bidder.

Ethan

That was what the message said... and as I read it shock slammed into my soul and froze my heart in my chest.

When Dorian flicked to the response from the sender I was ready to breathe fire:

I have a guy from North Korea. I'll get the prints from the mobster.

Leave it with me,

Balthazar

Dorian looked to me, the humor gone from his face.

"Is it something like this you're looking for? It tends to tick all the boxes," he remarked.

I couldn't even answer. I was just staring at the computer screen trying to process what I was reading.

Balthazar?

Ethan?

No...

It couldn't be true.

It couldn't.

Ethan wanted to take down Balthazar way back when, when I was part of the team. This didn't make any form of sense. But there was no mistake here.

Dorian switched the screen to another message from Ethan. This one had my name.

Ethan:

We need to move fast before The Chameleon takes the prints. Xander Cage is the only one I know who can get in and out of anywhere without being seen.

Balthazar:

Thought we killed that fucktard.

Ethan:

No he's still alive. He's in Brazil. I'll get him on board. He'll get the job done if I make the right promises.

I balled my fist and roared. I'd been fucking played. I'd been played.

Played by someone I fucking trusted.

Fuck. Fuck. Fuck!

Ethan… why?

This was on me for putting my trust in him. Me who made it my duty to trust no one.

Wes touched my elbow. His face a mixture of fury. He'd been played too.

But… wait…

This was…

I ran a hand through my hair and looked back to the message on the screen from Balthazar.

I thought we killed him.

He said *we…*

Oh God…

I backed away and stumbled against the chair behind me. This wasn't just a now thing, this game started years ago.

Ethan was responsible for everything. It was him… all of it.

The trap. The fucking trap in Nepal.

Claire… her death… it was him.

God… why didn't I see this? When Paul got captured protocol was to leave him. But it was a trap from then. We were a team, Ethan was our leader. He gave us the mission to go after Balthazar. Then it changed?

It was him. All along it was him.

He made the right promises for sure. My reward for getting the prints was five hundred grand and more importantly, a team assembled to help me find Balthazar.

But Ethan knew where to find him all along. As Giovanni said the person who'd contacted Balthazar would have just called him up for a chat.

This… This shit was exactly that.

Ethan and Balthazar…

Ethan and Balthazar working together…

"You okay pal?" Dorian asked, Wes knew not to ask me that.

I wanted to kill something, or someone, but on account of the help Dorian gave I thought I'd remember my manners and answer.

"No I'm not."

Wes suddenly tensed and snapped a worried gaze to me. "Xander, I just had a really bad thought. You know we were talking about how people would do things if they got desperate?"

"Yes." What the fuck now?

"Ethan knows I came to Idaho. I told him. He only left to meet up with his people this morning. Same time I left. Xander I told him where I was going. I'm sorry. I didn't know man." Panic filled his face. "He'd know about Jack right? We'd both assumed Jia was with you. Giovanni might still have the prints Xander, and if he doesn't he knows where they went. What if Ethan comes here and takes Jia? What if –"

Before he could even get the next words out his mouth I was on the move.

Him in tow behind me.

What if Ethan came here and took Jia?

Yes… that was the last thing left to do. The desperate thing, the last resort.

Wes was right.

If Giovanni didn't have the prints he would know where they went. The only way he'd cough up information like that would be to take the thing that was most important to him.

His prize.

His most prized possession.

Giovanni's most prized possession just happened to be the same as mine.

Her.

Jia.

CHAPTER 11

Jia

"I LOVE any kind of fruit in cake," I told Jack.

He smiled and shook his head. "Not me. I just like blueberries. I loathe raspberries, because of the seeds. I don't like anything that gets stuck in my teeth." Jack replied.

"I like to eat." Frankie intoned with a smirk and rubbed his belly.

I rolled my eyes at him. He was acting like he had an actual belly, like a pot belly. But he rubbed his hand over a six pack.

Jack just laughed when he saw my face.

"Well if you can look like that and eat cake then there's no complaint. I'm an old man, I have to watch myself."

"You don't look that old to me." I smiled.

"You're very sweet. I'll write that in my memoirs."

I giggled. "You have memoirs?"

"Yes, when you live as many lives as mine you have to document something. It would be a crime not to."

"Xander talks about his missions. It sounds really dangerous."

"Yes, well mine were roughly the same. No walk in the park, and no tea party. You live to tell the tale and you know you've lived."

"Sounds like my every day," Frankie scuffed as if it was nothing.

Jack paused and cut him a crude glance. "I'm sorry, have you been captured by Vietnamese resistants and held captive in a coffin filled with shards of broken glass while they throw fire ants all over you to try and get you to talk?"

My lips parted, Frankie just stared.

"No, fuck no, bro. Shit, that happened to you?" Frankie looked him over.

Jack nodded. "Yeah, but that wasn't the worst thing. I don't talk about the worst things."

And I took that to mean we shouldn't ask.

"That's horrible. I can't believe people would be so

cruel. Evil." Why was I even saying that? Pa would do that. It was just the sort of thing Pa would do. He'd love the fire ants idea to no end.

"It happens Princess."

He passed me the cupcake holders to choose which I wanted.

I took the pink ones and gave my mixture another good mix.

"So, this is what you do now?" Frankie asked. "Stay home and bake cookies? Doesn't seem to suit you."

"No, I work as a consultant for national security. I don't get a lot of work but when I do it's sufficient."

"*Sufficient?* I hope you mean that in a monetary way."

"I do. It pays well."

"Six figures?"

I glared at Frankie. "Frankie that's so rude. You can't ask him that."

"It's okay," Jack cut in. "The money varies depending on the job, but I aim for as close as possible to seven figures as I can. I know my worth."

Frankie looked impressed. "Fuck yeah. Say, do you think the US government could use a guy like me? Maybe I could be your assistant and assist you."

"Frankie, what the hell?" I placed my hands on my hips.

"Look girly, in case you didn't notice, I'm out of a

job and I can't exactly go back to Vegas." He raised his brows.

I would have continued my stance but he was right and it brought the guilt back.

We were here because of me, and realistically what the hell was Frankie supposed to do? Go to Brazil with us on the run?

Jesus.

As exciting as it all sounded it was farfetched.

Farfetched and sketchy like everything else. We were all doing our best here but my worry was just increasing with every passing second. There were too many variables but I was sure one would lead Pa here. I just knew it.

"Well maybe you could be your own boss. You're good in everything you do," I praised him with a little smile. I felt he deserved something nice along those lines since he really had stuck his neck out for me.

He nodded firmly with a wide smile plastered on his face. It made his beard look thicker. Usually he'd have it trimmed up but I was liking the more rugged look.

"I like that. I could be my own boss. Speaking of which, I gotta make a call." He straightened up.

"To home?"

"Thereabouts, don't worry, if something had happened I would tell you. No point keeping secrets now. If I think anyone is on the way here, you'll know by me grabbing you and heading for the truck."

I nodded even though I imagined him doing something more like throwing me over his shoulder and running to the truck with me.

"I have eyes in the sky," Jack stated. "People keeping tabs on the area. You'll know when we need to make a move."

That did sound more promising. I didn't know he had people watching like that.

"Thank you."

Frankie nodded his thanks and headed out the kitchen door, leaving me with Jack.

This was actually the first time that we'd been left by ourselves.

I didn't miss the tension that coiled around my heart.

It was from that awkwardness again of being here, it being clear that Xander and I were together and me feeling like the replacement.

"So, you manage to do anything with that sketch pad? I was looking for some paint but what I found dried up several moons ago," Jack said with a little chuckle.

He was trying to make me feel at ease. I could tell.

"I drew last night. Sometimes that's okay."

"Well we can run to the store tomorrow and get

some stuff if you like. The surroundings are beautiful this time of year."

"Thank you, I would really love that. Everything here is beautiful. Did you paint?" I asked only because he'd mentioned the paint that dried up.

The shift in his mood however showed it wasn't him that used to paint and I'd asked yet another question I shouldn't have.

"Not me. It was my daughter," Jack answered and the guilt just intensified.

"I'm sorry. I … shouldn't have asked."

He chuckled surprising me. "Jia, it's okay… and for heavens sakes you don't have to walk around tense because you're with Xander. It's good you two found each other, no matter the circumstances. I can tell he cares very much for you and I just hope this whole incident gets resolved as soon as. Happiness is always a great outcome."

"Thank you. I appreciate that. I care deeply for him too. I wish I could be more useful. I wish this wasn't about me. I wish my father wasn't so…" There was so much to wish for when it came to Pa. So damn much. "I just wish he was normal. Not the mafia boss. He was normal sometimes. When he cooked."

"He cooks?"

"Yeah, he always insists on fresh everything and bringing the Italian cuisine to the table, like he's bringing *Italia* itself. My mother was the same. Cooking. For me it's the one thing we do that brings people together. Everybody loves good food, right?"

He smiled at that. "I agree. I love cooking. I insisted on teaching my daughter how to cook but just like everything else, she refused to learn. Why learn when you could have take out or me doing cuisine meals?"

I laughed. Xander couldn't cook either.

"So you were the cook?"

"I was the cook and the bearer of failed attempts. So when she decided she wanted to do art I got her everything she asked for only for her to give up a week later, when she decided she wanted to do ballet so she could be more like the other girls. I got her the whole caboodle, tutu and all. She hated that with a fiery passion. One day I told her to just do what she loved. She joined the air cadets. Then followed my career path like it was a road map."

"Wow. That is amazing." I loved how he spoke so highly of her. "I'm sure she was amazing."

"She was and she died doing what she loved most. The memories keep her alive for me. Death is the risk we take with jobs like ours. But we wouldn't do it if we didn't think it was worth it."

I nodded. "Yes. I agree. It's so honorable and beautiful. I hope I can be something worthwhile like that one day. All my life everything was given to me, art is the only thing that I do where I get to show my heart and who I am."

"Miss Jia, I swear to God I'm looking at you right now and I can see your heart and who you are. Don't worry about things like that. Enjoy life and try not to..." His voice trailed off when his phone buzzed in his pocket.

He reached for it at the same time that Frankie ran back in the kitchen, guns in both hands.

"Guys we have company, doesn't look like our people," Frankie balked. "Two guys on bikes were heading toward the house from the woods."

My heart jumped in my throat and I dropped the mixing spoon.

Oh God no...

What was happening?

Jack whipped out his phone and spoke to someone really quick.

"Ra. They're here. We have to get out of here," Jack cried. He moved to the cupboard and pulled out a gun.

Just then though, a loud smash echoed in the sitting room and two men ran into the kitchen.

Jack fired a shot from the smaller gun and took them out.

He then grabbed my hands and put me behind him while we moved forward, Frankie next to us, just in time to see more guys filling the house.

Jack shoved me in the corner and opened the door to the basement.

"Go down there and stay there until I say," he ordered.

I did as he said, following exactly what he said.

I opened the door and ran down the stairs.

After five minutes I wasn't sure what was worse for me, being upstairs and in the action where maybe I could have helped, but also get myself killed. Or being down here and listening.

Gun fire clashes, then thuds would echo over the roof as bodies went down.

People would scream in pain, scream to take cover, then scream as they died.

It went on like that for maybe fifteen minutes, but it felt like forever.

It was like a forever of the horrible sounds above me, then something changed. The sounds were still there but I swore I heard the door open from the back of the house.

I did. Next came heavy footsteps. Several people came in then my heart squeezed when the door to the basement opened.

I didn't think Jack would be coming down here with the gunfire still going. So it could only have been someone else.

I ran behind the washing machine and hid there. It

was the best place I could find with so little time to react. I hadn't expected anyone to come down here, but why wouldn't they?

I was so stupid.

Now was not the time to be stupid either dealing with these people.

The Ra...

Christ, what would they want? What the hell would they want? Xander didn't have the prints but maybe they thought he got them.

Balthazar knew that Xander knew where to find them so this was retaliation.

Shit.

A pair of legs came into view where I could see.

There was another and another.

Then damn it, another, but these legs wore suit pants quite unlike the other guys who wore cargo pants.

The suit guy moved forward and it was like he just knew where to look. Maybe I was completely obvious.

Maybe I was foolish. I should have covered myself or something. It would have been better than perching behind the washing machine.

Because that was the first place Balthazar Kane looked and the smile that filled his face when he saw me made my blood freeze.

CHAPTER 12

Xander

No!

Not again.

I was too late.

I was too fucking late.

Wes and I pulled up at the house and it looked like disaster had struck. There were military officials outside, walking around. They tried to stop me but I pushed ahead, running inside.

I got to the living room and found a battered and bloodied Jack on the floor, with paramedics tending to him. He was out cold. No sign of Jia.

I rushed up to Jack. He looked bad.

"I'm sorry we have to tend to him." The paramedic said to me.

Frankie came around and Wes joined us.

"I'm sorry man. We were ambushed," Frankie began. He looked like he'd taken a beating too. But the beating he got wouldn't have been enough to give him the sadness in his eyes. "Xander it was Ra guys and they took Jia. We thought she was in the basement. I was out here covering your old man."

I walked over to the wall and threw a punch into the concrete.

"I'm sorry," he said.

"Not your fault. Not yours."

"Xander calm down. Please." Wes winced.

I looked over to Jack, he started coughing when he came to. I rushed back to him and he saw me. His left eye was so swollen and bruised he couldn't open it, but he reached out to me.

"Boy they took her. It was Balthazar. He was here."

My skin buzzed from the trauma. It was all just getting worse and worse.

Balthazar was here, so Wes was spot on in his assumption of what would happen next.

Fuck. It was all so fucking convenient that I wasn't here.

"I'm sorry Jack. Fuck, I'm sorry." Once again I felt useless. Fucking useless as shit.

"Save the sorrys boy. I'm okay but we have to get her back. You find out anything useful from Dorian?" It was typical Jack to be in business mode even in this state.

"It was Ethan. It was him all along. He played me, he played me for years too. He and Balthazar were in cahoots. It's on him why Claire died, Jack."

Jack growled and tried to get up but the paramedic pressed a firm hand down on him.

"Ethan!" Jack cried. "That fucking dog! He'll pay."

Pay?

He was the reason why Claire had been killed and now the same thing could happen to Jia. I didn't doubt that one bit. Right now though it didn't look like I was in any position to be making any threats.

What the fuck was I going to do?

Balthazar had Jia.

Balthazar had my girl.

We sent out a search party.

The best kind of people that Jack had at his fingertips.

No one found a trace of them.

It was like Jia had just disappeared. Completely

gone. What I called off grid. I shouldn't have been surprised. Wasn't I used to dealing with Balthazar and the Ra? I knew how the fucking man worked. I knew how he treated people he kidnapped.

I kept seeing images in my mind. Images of Claire's body. Her being shot, blood splattered then the explosion. Death.

That was what this meant. And time was passing.

I'd looked with the guys too, we went further than the state line and decided they had to have gone out of state.

They really had all the power. Jack told me the place had been flooded with men. Men came on bikes and cars, but there was no trace, nothing picked up on any camera.

I knew what that was, they'd made sure they screwed with all cameras that could pick them up on their route. That was the best explanation I could come up with. It had to be that because that was unheard of.

Time was passing and we were nowhere nearer than we'd been when I first got back to the house.

I didn't sleep and when morning came the next day I couldn't believe Jia really wasn't with me. I couldn't believe it.

In my cynical mind I cursed myself. Her father wanted to send her to Italy with Armand so she would be safe.

I stopped that from happening. My intervention stopped her from being somewhere she would have been safe.

I was here sitting on my ass without a paddle of an idea on what to do next other than try the most lamest of things.

I tried calling Ethan.

I'd done it yesterday too.

I tried calling him as a last resort. Not really thinking I was going to get an answer.

The same fucking thing happened now.

The phone rang out to voicemail so I ended the call. I'd left him enough messages for him to know what it was I wanted. I doubted though that I would have needed to say anything.

The hours that followed since we got back felt like eons, and now I was sitting on the front porch with a cigarette in my hand. It was one of Jack's. I hadn't smoked in years but this right now was something I needed to calm me down because everything had blown up in my face. Everything.

I glanced down at my watch, it was nearly nine.

It rained last night so there was a slight mist about the place and it wasn't as bright as it usually was at this hour of the morning. The scenery suited my mood.

Jack opened the door and came out. He had a slight limp and his arm was in a sling.

He'd broken a few ribs yesterday and taken a bullet to his shoulder but it passed through at an angle that probably hurt like a bitch but wouldn't leave too much damage. He'd been told to stay in the hospital for a few days. Jack being Jack however stayed long enough to get patched up with some stitches and discharged himself straight after.

He said staying in like that was for people who had nothing better to do and as long as he could move he was leaving and coming to help me.

He pulled out his lighter, lit up, and held the flame to me when I got out another cigarette. Jack then reached for a cigar from his back pocket and lit it up.

He sat opposite me on the porch, gazing out into the open the same way I was.

"I'm sorry Xander," he said, voice just above a whisper.

I shook my head and looked at him.

"No, you have nothing to be sorry for," I told him.

"I feel like shit. You asked me to watch her and she got taken on my watch. I had eyes in the sky and everything. She still got taken." He took a draw on his cigar and blew out the smoke in a ring. "If it wasn't for your friend Frankie I would have been a goner. They blindsided me big time and tried to undercut me. He had my back. We thought she'd be safe in the basement. They went down there and I don't even know when they took her. There was no scream or anything. They just took her."

"I need to get her back Jack. I have to. I can't allow Balthazar to …" I couldn't say the words.

He wouldn't just kill her.

He wouldn't.

He'd told me so himself when he went to her house. He knew what she meant to me and the things he said were the kind that were enough to make me end him if he didn't have a gun pointed at her.

"Don't think like that, son. Don't. We just have to hope."

I tossed the cigarette and redialed Ethan's number.

Another fruitless attempt maybe, but it was what I had. We had Dorian track the number but it came up with somewhere listed in Vegas. Around the area we'd been when we were there. We knew then that he couldn't have been anywhere near us because he was hours away.

It suggested he'd ditched the phone.

I hung up when the same fucking thing happened as before. But unlike before, my phone rang and it was an unrecognized number.

I answered straight away.

"Who is this?" I barked.

"Xander Cage is that any way to answer the phone? Really?" It was Ethan!

Jack straightened up instantly as I bolted up.

"Ethan, where the fuck are you? Where is Jia?" I was just talking. Not quite thinking about what the hell it was I was asking him.

Realistically I wanted to kill him. I wanted to kill him.

"Xander, I tried so hard to hide the truth from you. I really did. But it was to no avail. I suppose these things come out eventually. The way things were going meant they had to at some point."

I seethed, trying hard to focus on the right thing to say.

"It was you. All of it. All along. It was you. Right from the damn start. You. When? When did you switch sides?"

Everything was tumbling through my mind. I wanted answers for all of it.

He cleared his throat. "Is that really relevant now?"

"Yes, you will tell me and then you're going to tell me where Jia is."

"Old friend, this is a courtesy call. Not one where you make demands. It's one to tell you to give up the chase. We're seeking other avenues now. The same way you like to get in and out and not leave a trace, the same way I like to be clean, not leave any baggage behind or shit that can follow you. I was the one who insisted on not taking her for leverage at the start. I really thought you would have stolen the prints and everything would have run smoothly. It might have worked if you hadn't gotten involved with the girl. It clouded your judgment Xander and your ability to do your job. You got messy, you slipped up, you weren't thinking straight. This is the result."

"Son of a bitch, tell me where she is."

"No. Like I said, I won't be doing that. We'll do things the dirty way from here onwards. She is leverage, so we'll see just how important she is to Giovanni Marchesi. I guess though I can tell you when it was I changed sides." He chuckled. "The truth is, I was always who I was. I was always part of The Ra. I'm a leader, just like Balthazar. The thing about leadership in The Ra is that we never wear the mark. The same way he doesn't have any tattoos on him to give him away as a Spade or even part of The Ra, is the same way I am. It's how we work. I worked my way in to get the intel. All the things I needed to get to report to my superiors. Years of work. We infiltrate and become part of the system until we need to strike. That's how we're always one step ahead of the game."

My God.

That was exactly it. That was why it felt like Balthazar was always ahead. It felt like that because he was, he absolutely fucking was.

Ethan was the Joker Giovanni referred to when he

tortured me. Giovanni, that asshole. He knew too that it had to be someone like Ethan that had sent me. That was why he asked the questions. I was such an idiot. I was such a fucking fool.

Fucking hell.

"How can you think this was all okay? We all trusted you. Me, Claire, Paul, Lucas, John. The Shadow unit, we trusted you." That was the name given to the unit because of me, because I moved like a shadow. "*You* formed the unit to hunt the Ra." That was the fucking irony in it.

"I did but only as a request from the ministry of defense. That wasn't me. It came about as a response to The Ra becoming more dangerous. I just positioned myself so I'd be in charge of you. I knew if I had control over a unit like yours then I'd know who'd be hunting my people and where they'd be. Then you guys got good. Better than good. We had to find a way to eradicate you. But you got away, Xander Cage. You got away. And just when I thought you might be useful to me, you proved me wrong. You were useless. We should have just gone for the girl in the first place. Well, we have her now."

My chest tightened up with fury and all the angst from the last five years. I was the one who wanted answers and vengeance. Right now I didn't know if I could handle hearing the confession of what really took place. I couldn't believe I'd allowed this man to fool me.

"You'll pay for this Ethan. You evil piece of shit, you'll pay. Mark my word." I turned to see Jack, who'd been looking on at me and listening in. He nodded his agreement at my words.

"Your threats mean nothing to me. It falls on deaf ears. Water on a ducks back. Anyhow, like I said, this is a courtesy call. Something in the way of wrapping things up."

"Bastard…" I could have breathed fire. I squeezed the phone so hard I thought I might possibly break it. I couldn't believe the treachery.

Fuck, what an asshole. He was working both sides all along and none of us could see it. Even Jack had known him from way back when.

"Yes, I am exactly that Xander. I'm a fucking bastard. Anyway, much as I'd love to chat, I have to go. This is really goodbye. My advice to you is to let sleeping dogs lie. You weren't supposed to get involved. Maybe you should back away now."

"Back away, are you kidding me?"

"Goodbye old friend." He hung up.

Just like that, he hung up.

He fucking hung up and there was no damn number to call or trace. That was it, a bid of farewell to tell me shit about giving up.

I looked to Jack again but then I spotted a black Sedan approaching the driveway.

Jack ran inside and grabbed two guns. One for him, one for me.

Whoever this motherfucker was, they certainly had a death wish.

They seriously thought they could park up on the drive and come for us again?

No fucking way.

Jack and I walked down the steps guns ready to fire.

The Sedan stopped and I pulled the trigger back.

Who I saw step out of the car shocked me to shit.

Giovanni.

He'd driven.

He was driving the car and there was no one else with him. He looked like hell. Like he'd been on a bender.

He reached into the car and from the passenger seat he pulled out the all too familiar to me tube that contained the blueprints.

The fucking blueprints.

The thing this whole saga was about.

He held them up in the air, pulled his gun from his back pocket and tossed it on the ground.

The man shocked me further by walking up to us and holding out the prints for me to take.

The last time I was this close to him he'd been

torturing me. He'd dropped a queen of hearts playing card on the floor before me and told me it was Jia.

Yes, he was right. She was the queen of both our hearts.

Now he was staring me down, and looked me deep in the eye.

"They have my little girl." He spoke and his eyes clouded. "They want the prints in exchange for her, but I know how this works. I won't get her back alive. I need you to help me get her back because you're the only person in this world who loves her as much as me."

A tear ran down his cheek and the Vegas king pulled the queen of hearts from his jacket pocket and held it before me.

I lowered my gun.

CHAPTER 13

Jia

My head...

Why the hell did it feel like it was going to explode?

Fall off, and explode.

I had the distinct memory of being back at college at that frat party. Maybe I was still there.

Billy Taylor put something in my drink. I was sure of it. We were playing poker at the frat house and he'd been trying to get me to go out with him for weeks, but I was more interested in Jake Harvey, the Sigma Kappa vice president. I'd had my eye on him for weeks, but he didn't know that.

He also didn't know that I was only at that party to check him out.

My plan backfired though when I'd started feeling sick and the room started spinning. Billy took me to his room and started taking my clothes off. Then Jake came and stopped him.

I remembered it, and remembered it happen. I also remembered that I ended up in hospital because whatever the fuck he'd given me made me so sick I was down for weeks.

When I got back to college I was told he'd just disappeared. No one had seen or heard of him again.

That was the workings of Pa...

My eyes fluttered open and the bright light pierced into them like the bright rays of the sun, far too bright and it wasn't sunlight.

Where was I?

Where the hell was I?

This wasn't college. That already happened, and Pa had told me I wouldn't have to worry about Billy anymore.

No one ever saw or heard from him again. The thought twisted my insides because I didn't know what happened to him. Was he dead or alive? Pa never told me. He wouldn't.

It tore at my insides for years.

It tore at me even as I thought about it now.

Pa did something to him.

It wasn't, however, something I could worry about now or any other time, that was eight years ago. And I was here, wherever this place was and the memories of what had happened to me were starting to filter into my mind.

Balthazar Kane had captured me. I'd tried to save myself. I remembered all the horrible things he said to me and tried to save myself, then someone grabbed me from behind and covered my mouth with a cloth that contained something strong and pungent. Some kind of knock out solution like chloroform.

It felt like I'd been out cold for days.

I squinted against the light and pried my eyes open again. I lifted my head and looked around me at the four white walls that greeted me. The place looked like one of those cells you'd see in a psychiatric hospital minus the bed. Instead of the bed was the chair I was sitting on, with my hands tied to my back.

That was as much as I knew.

The door creaked and the round handle turned.

I shuffled up straight so I could see who was coming in and tried not to look so helpless.

The sight of the man who came in made me gasp.

That was... his name was Ethan. He wore a black patch over his eye. I remembered him from the ware-house back in Vegas where I'd seen Xander. That was when I first found out who Xander was. This man was talking to him, giving him orders. He'd told him he might have to kill me.

What was going on?

I thought the Ra guys had taken me. Balthazar...

So why was he here?

"You look like you know me." He observed, looking me over.

"I don't know you. We've never met. Let me go now!" I demanded.

He laughed. He looked at me and laughed like I'd actually said something funny.

"That's not how this works, Miss Marchesi. You see, my people need you. Your father has something we need and you're the way we'll be getting it."

I saw it now.

I understood.

He wasn't who people thought he was. So many players in this game wearing masks. He'd double crossed Xander. I was sure of it.

"You're part of the Ra and part of the team Xander works for. Didn't think you could do both."

He smiled. "Thought you didn't know me. I wonder when it was you found out about a mission that should have been secret. He told you, didn't he?"

"He didn't tell me anything. I saw for myself and

kept the secret. How could you do this? Those prints are for nukes. The Ra are terrorists."

"You say that like you think I'm under some kind of spell. As one of the Ra leaders I'm very aware of what they represent."

My mouth fell open. He was one of The Ra leaders. Jesus. We were all doomed from the beginning.

He laughed when he saw my reaction, moved closer and resumed his speech. "Terrorist is such a strong word, watch how you use it. Put simply, we go where the money is. We enable. We make the unimaginable possible and force leaders to bend to our will. It's not always by the gun that you get people to listen to you. *Science.* That is power." He tapped the side of his head. "Science and knowledge are formidable when combined. You have the key, you can open the door then anything can happen. Anything you want if you make it possible. That is what we do, we're just ruthless bastards."

"What do you want with the blueprints?" It was a question that was irrelevant to my situation but I needed to know what it was all for. The why of it.

I just wanted to know what had led me here.

"War. It's on the horizon. Countries get antsy and start slipping when there is unrest and they can't come to an agreement on what to do, and who to side with. That's when the most powerful countries start making back up plans. They contact people like us to get hold of something that gives them the upper hand. This time we did the choosing based on previous clientele who offered us a billion dollars. That is how much the blueprints are worth to them."

I'd only heard of such things in the movies or the news. Wild and bizarre. As he'd spoken I had the sensation of hearing him but not quite believing he was talking to me or believing what he was saying.

I thought Pa was evil...

What about a man who worked for the government? Xander was under the impression that he was doing this mission to prevent the prints from getting into the wrong hands.

I couldn't imagine what would have happened if he'd actually been successful and handed them over.

It didn't matter now because look at me.

"You should be ashamed of yourself," I spat. It sounded stupid to say. It was the sort of thing my great aunt Layla would say and everyone would laugh because she sounded so ridiculous trying to tell off a bunch of mafia guys.

Ethan laughed now. I guess I sounded the same, trying to point shame on an anarchist.

Fuck him for laughing. I didn't care, he was getting my opinion whether he liked it or not, and whether it meant anything to him or not. He could go fuck himself.

"Asshole, you'll get yours and I hope you fucking die a painful death."

"Wow, looks like she has balls."

"Yeah? Guess what, you may think you can lure my father here and he'll do whatever you say because you have me, but you messed with the wrong people. We're the Marchesis, you prick. My father may give you what you want but you might not be alive to enjoy it or see that fucking plan of yours come to be."

He didn't like me saying that.

"We will see about that. We really will, Miss Marchesi, for your sake I hope Daddy dearest will comply and come willingly. We have our ways here. If he doesn't then I'm sure you'll be useful in some other way."

As he said that I spotted someone at the door. Outside the door. I hadn't noticed before that it was one of those with the little sliding window that allowed you to pull it across.

It was one of those and Balthazar Kane stood outside it just watching. Watching me.

Looking at me with those cold calculative eyes that made me want to run and hide forever.

I'd never met anyone who could instill the fear of God in me with just one look. It was that sort of wild, maddening, psychotic look of a person who'd done wrong. A lot of wrong and in the worst of ways.

The way he spoke to me when we first met. Telling me that he'd fuck me as many times as he could before he killed me.

Who said things like that?

Who thought it was okay to say things like that?

Men like him.

I wished for Xander. I wished with all my heart for Xander.

Chances were I'd never see him again.

This would be it for me.

This would be my end.

This would be my end whether Pa brought the prints and did as they said or not.

CHAPTER 14

Xander

"WHAT ARE YOU DOING?" Giovanni asked. He looked to me with those sharp eyes assessing what I was doing.

"I'll ask the questions here," I answered, sharpening my gaze on him.

I'd already agreed to do whatever I had to, to get Jia back, even if I had to sign my damn life away to the devil, or work with him.

We'd gone inside the house. When Frankie saw him he nearly shit himself. Wes turned pale. Literally sheet pale.

KHARDINE GRAY

Both men exhibited reactions that were understandable because this was the guy who'd sent us here.

I might have lowered my gun but Jack kept his pointed at my old boss while I laid out the blueprints on the dinner table to go over them.

I took them out of the tube to make sure everything was as it should be.

Everything in accordance with the way they were detailed in my mission brief.

I wouldn't have put it past this son of a bitch to come with shit and try to trick me so he could get Jia and then try to steal her away from me.

I wouldn't have put such a thing past him but these looked like the real deal. When I'd taken them out of the glass case in the secret chamber I never got the chance to look inside before he came and captured me.

Screwed me over more like.

I stopped pouring over them and looked at him.

We'd gathered in the dining room because of the table and the bigger space to bounce ideas.

In the room were Jack, Wes, Frankie, Giovanni, me, and Dorian. Dorian had come by a few minutes ago. Jack had called him earlier. He was probably expecting to come and help with something technical and happened upon our little standoff here, with Giovanni sitting in the armchair looking like he was getting ready to read the Sunday paper while Jack's shotgun aimed at his head.

Badass. That's what he was.

He knew, he knew no matter what stance I took or what I did or said, I'd do whatever he asked if it helped me save Jia.

He knew I was in love with his daughter and I supposed he knew too not to fuck with me.

So far he'd said he was waiting on the call from Balthazar with the details of where to make the exchange. He'd only made contact and offered Jia up for the prints. That was all that had happened so far.

It was a lot, but there were so many other questions swirling around in my mind.

"How were you able to bring these to us? I was under the impression that you'd handed them over to The Chameleon."

"I was supposed to, then you took Jia and we never got the chance to meet for the exchange. With people after the prints they aren't something you just hand over in the conventional sense."

"So that's it, he won't come here with God knows who after you?"

"He is not my concern. I was very clear from the beginning when I got onboard this shit show that my family shouldn't have been placed in danger."

I remembered that conversation with him.

"There was never any way to control that." I threw back. It pissed me off to no end whenever I heard people got themselves into deep shit and it blew up in their faces, dragging their loved ones into it, then they'd say they didn't know it would come to this or that their actions would end up causing any harm.

It was all bullshit. No matter which way it went, this started with him and what he agreed to do.

"Maybe so."

That answer wasn't good enough. "Giovanni, don't fuck with me. Tell me now if you think The Chameleon or anybody else will follow your ass here."

He grit his teeth. It was clear he hated the switch in power. "He will not. He thinks I'm still in Vegas. He has no idea what's happened. I was to arrange to meet with him in the week to make the exchange. That is all."

Good. Then the damn Chameleon wasn't my concern either. If we got out of this, I'd hand the blueprints over to Jack and he could give them to the right people. That was what I'd decided.

"Fine." I kept my gaze trained on Giovanni who was still staring at me.

"There's still stuff you need to tell me too, Xander Cage. Did you ever work out who the joker was? I still can't." He gave me a wicked smirk. The menace behind it suggested he knew I knew by now that I'd been played.

"Ethan Ranger, the man who hired me. It was him," I replied keeping my tone even to tamp down my rage.

Giovanni smiled and started clapping. "Sometimes I really love myself. I have a beautiful mind. You know, had you told me something I would have figured it out. I would have figured out that someone was playing us. And you're an agent."

"I am not. I was doing a job I thought was for the greater good. I didn't realize I was just another piece in a game. A pawn." I intensified my glare on him. Frankie mentioned the Russian government as the leads in charge of the whole operation. Now was a perfect time to get answers. "What about you? Who were you holding these for?" I waved my hand over the blueprints.

"Does it matter?"

"If I didn't want to know I wouldn't ask the question." Actually it didn't matter one fuck, but it added to the details of what I knew.

"The Presidency of Russia," he answered, sharing. Actually telling me. Frankie heard right.

"Okay. Now we know the back story. Do you have any idea where they might have taken Jia?" It was time for action. We'd talked enough about shit we couldn't do anything about.

Giovanni shook his head. "Not a damn clue. I have no idea. For all I know they could be in Timbuktu. The only consolation I have is that they'd have to move with the speed of light to get there. I just have to wait for the call."

"They'll be watching," Jack suddenly said.

Giovanni looked to him. "Of course they will. Those people never stop watching. They know I'm here but do not care about that. They just want the prints. That is all. They don't care about the details, that is the power of The Ra."

I wish to God we were dealing with anyone else besides them, anybody else.

Fucking hell.

A shiver ran down my spine when his phone started buzzing.

He reached for it and answered it.

I had my eyes peeled on him but out the corner of my eye I noticed Dorian pull something from his pocket too.

"Hello," Giovanni said into the phone. He pressed it to his ear. His face hardened and my heart sped up its beat to a hundred miles an hour.

It was beating so fast as I waited.

"I will see you then," Giovanni stated and hung up. He grit his teeth and growled. "Twin Falls. They want me to come to Twin Falls at noon tomorrow with prints. I get to the civic center and they'll send a fucking address."

QUEEN OF HIS HEART

"I got the address," Dorian announced, pulling our attention to him.

"What?" I asked.

He held up the device he'd taken out earlier. It looked like one of those battery charger units but it had a more slimline look to it.

He smiled. "My device tracked them within seconds."

"It said unrecognized number on my phone," Giovanni stated widening his eyes.

Dorian waved his hand as if that was nothing. "Ugh, that's nothing lad. I can get round that piss easy with my wee device, so much the better when they're live in conversation for longer than a minute. I picked up your number when you got here and set my device to track any number that made contact with you."

I knew I would like this guy. A plan was brewing in my mind.

"Dorian, can we locate the address and hack the systems? Do you have anything like that?" I asked. "I'd just need something to rewrite a few algorithms and codes."

Dorian smiled. "Now you're speaking my language."

"Perfect. Now we have a plan."

"Care to let me in on that plan?" Giovanni asked.

"Sure. We're not getting anywhere for noon tomorrow. We're getting there before sunrise, before the dawn of the new fucking day. If we can check out the location we know what we're doing and where we're going. We go in and get Jia."

"I have to take the prints in case it goes wrong. I won't sacrifice my daughter for them." He pointed to the prints. "I won't do it, I don't care what they're worth."

For the first time since this storm happened, I actually respected the guy.

"We take the prints but we're leaving with her, *alive*." I nodded. "Wes I need you with Dorian to be my eyes." I looked over at Wes who gave me both thumbs up.

"Eyes like an eagle bro."

"Frankie stay here with Jack."

Both men looked at me like I was crazy.

"Are you insane? I'm not letting you go on this mission by yourself." Jack protested.

"I won't be by myself. Giovanni's coming with me."

Giovanni straightened and focused his gaze on me.

"The two of you can't just go on this suicide mission by yourselves. I won't allow it," Jack flared. He lowered his gun on Giovanni and stared me down. The wealth of seriousness mingled with worry in his eyes.

It was times like these when I was grateful to have someone who cared for me. Wes was my best friend, but it was different. I wondered how it was I'd lived without it for the last five years. It was the same as how

I wondered how I'd existed for the first sixteen years of my life without him and Claire.

"Jack, you are injured, badly."

"Like fuck am I injured. You are … you are my son. You are like a son to me and I just got you back. I'm coming whether you fucking like it or not."

When Jack spoke there was no point arguing. I could imagine me trying to talk him out of it and then just getting pushed back. I gave him a curt nod, agreeing. I supposed the more muscle we had the better.

"Okay."

"I'll assemble some guys," Jack added. Hope filled me when he said that because I knew he meant guys who were like twenty of me.

"Thank you."

"I'm coming too," Frankie chimed in. "Don't expect me to sit here and scratch my ass until you come back."

Giovanni gave him the same hard look he had when he first came in and saw him.

"How touching. All aboard. *Traitor*," Giovanni hissed.

I was glad when Frankie made his way over to him and squared off with him.

"I don't care what the hell you call me *boss*," Frankie countered. "I'm not the traitor, you are. To your country. Greedy mobster, getting in shit and not getting all the details. The fine print."

The look in Giovanni's eyes hardened. "That is none of your concern," he answered.

"You get involved with something like that, sacrifice your best men and now look where your daughter is."

"Frankie, she wouldn't be in danger if you didn't take her," Giovanni countered. The sting of his words got me.

Frankie shook his head though.

"It wouldn't matter where you sent her, those people would have found her. Send her to the moon and they would find her. Believe me, it was inevitable no matter where she went. Armand, that asshole would have saved himself first before her if shit had gone down in Italy. And your family there are no match for The Ra. Your people here or there are no match for them. It's the reason why you're here." Frankie stepped back away from him but wasn't finished with him yet. "Be grateful she was taken somewhere where we still have a chance to do something about it."

I wouldn't excuse the guilt I felt that Jia had been taken, and it didn't make me feel any better to hear she still would have been taken, his words held truth though. They held truth and I was listening and paying attention. Grateful for his wisdom.

This was our chance. My chance that I wouldn't blow this time.

"Okay guys, let's do this. We'll assemble in a few hours and get this done. Get her back," I stated.

I was looking at Giovanni, who'd resumed his former worry. He'd resumed the worried sick father mode.

Worried sick didn't begin to describe my worry.

I knew what Balthazar Kane was like.

No one here, aside from me, had seen the extent of his madness first hand.

I was really praying there wouldn't be a repeat of it.

CHAPTER 15

Jia

I'D BEEN WATCHING everyone's movements. Watching what they did and how they operated.

Their process.

What I was looking for was a way of escaping.

Yes...

I'd officially put my hand up and admit that I'd gone bat shit crazy.

But then, I was pretty sure there were a few times in my life when I'd said the same thing.

This time was just the time that really mattered and it needed my craziness to push the limits so I could believe in myself. Believe I could do this.

Escape this place.

It started with this room. if I could get out of the room then I could have some type of chance. Maybe…

I had to try. I had to.

I couldn't just allow Balthazar to do whatever he wanted to me. I couldn't sit here and wait and accept my fate.

It was crazy.

That would be crazy. Not trying would be crazy and the coward's way out.

Ethan hadn't come back since I spoke to him. That was many hours ago. I even fell asleep. What put me in gear for this plan of mine was waking up to seeing Balthazar watching me. It was so creepy. So damn creepy and gave me that instant feeling of some violation although he hadn't touched me.

That had been some hours ago too.

They had a guard at the door, who'd taken me to the toilet twice already. It was down the corridor from the room. I'd gone the second time to get another look at the place. There was a vent in the wall above the toilet. I was hoping to go in there and try and get gone.

The time was now. It had to be now. I'd already been here too long.

"Guard!" I called out. "Guard!"

He was standing there on the outside of the door

ignoring me. *Idiot.* I wished I could be one of those women who could seriously handle themselves. Someone like Xena or fuck, Wonder Woman was needed to kick his ass and put him in his place. Actually, the whole fucking lot of them.

Since I was neither Xena, nor Wonder woman I would have to settle for what I could do, and that was to be as annoying as fuck.

I called him over and over again.

"Guard, guard, guard, guard, guarddddddddddddd!!!"

That got him good. The door practically flew open and he burst in eyes boring into me like daggers.

Now it was time to turn on the charm.

"I need the toilet," I said with a smile and lifted my shoulder into a sassy shrug.

"You just went," he snarled.

"That was hours ago. You want me to piss on the floor? I don't really care but I don't think you people want that do you?"

"This is some fucking joke," he huffed. I gathered babysitting duties weren't his usual thing.

He walked over to me and undid the ropes around my feet, my hands next.

This was the part where even if I knew some kind of self-defense I'd try to escape.

This guy would have me on the floor in seconds though if I tried anything like that. he was a military looking type that would have been fitting to Pa's knights. The kind of man who didn't fuck around and was not to be fucked with.

I stood when he grabbed my arm and started hustling me toward the door.

My legs wobbled from the non-activity for the last few hours and having to keep still.

We got to the little toilet cubicle and he allowed me to go inside. He'd only allowed me in by myself because it was so small and the toilet was right there.

The minute I got in and closed the door I knew I only had seconds. Seconds before he realized I'd gone. That meant that once I got inside the vent I had to power through and hope like hell it got me somewhere I could get out properly. I'd seen most vents like this lead outside. That was my hope. These were built to regulate the air flow in buildings so there had to be a path of sorts that led outside.

I turned on the tap and let it trickle so it would sound like I was peeing. Then I made a move. I stood on the toilet seat and moved to the sink. The vent was above. I pushed it in and thanked my lucky stars it was one of those flap style ones like what Pa had installed back in the hotel rooms at The Marchesi.

I didn't waste any time I hoisted myself up and pushed in with my head, sliding in and clawing my way up the slippery shaft.

Oh God… I was in.

I actually did it and it was small. Just small enough for me to make my way through. A big guy like the guard wouldn't have been able to fit. It wouldn't stop him though. It wouldn't fucking stop him if he decided to shoot me and then scoop me out after.

The freedom and adrenaline that rushed through me propelled me forward , scuttling down the path as fast as I could, and fucking faster when I heard the faint sounds of commotion from where I'd come from.

God all I'd had was about two minutes before he must have gone into the toilet and realized what I'd done.

I didn't allow it to faze me or throw me.

Keep going Jia. Keep going girl. You got this.

Christ… the echoes of voices outside the vent sent shivers down my spine. I couldn't do this. I couldn't. The best I could hope for was that the path truly led outside and in some miracle spot that would give me an opening to run.

I approached a section ahead where it split off into five different pathways. I followed my instinct for survival and went toward the one that had the most light.

More light may mean daylight. It might have helped if I knew what time of day it was. For all I knew that could have just been a very bright light.

It got brighter and looked like daylight.

I prayed it was.

Please God let it be daylight.

I pounded forward propelling my body to move. When I got to the end of the path and gazed out desperate to see some kind of greenery I frowned when I realized I'd just gone toward a room.

This had to be the way though. I'd have to take the route. I couldn't go backwards.

I pushed the vent panel open and pulled myself out.

There was about a ten foot drop to the floor. falling would be just like when I fell out of that tree at Great Auntie Layla's house when I was twelve.

That was an accident. This was survival but I fell the same way. With a loud thump, smacking into the floor.

That was one of the differences between then and now. The ground was a lot softer than a tiled floor.

The pain was the same.

The room was some kind of hall. A meeting room. There was a long table ahead of me that looked like it was used for a buffet and there were a few chairs dotted here and there.

All the while I looked around I still couldn't quite work out what sort of building this was. *A house? An office?*

Something else. what sort of house had the cell like

cubicle I'd been held in and vents like where I'd just crawled from?

It didn't matter. Whatever it was and wherever I was, I needed to get out.

I made a run for the doors, opened them and landed smack into a wall.

The impact made me rebound and recoil. I stumbled backwards but gathered my footing only to see that it wasn't a wall I crashed into.

It was Balthazar Kane.

Balthazar Kane. My worst nightmare.

"Oh my God…" I breathed.

"God will not help you here, sugar." He snarled and landed a slap straight across my face.

As the pain lanced through me stars speckled my vision.

Part of me thought I should have prepped for the slap.

In the last few weeks I'd been slapped twice. In my life no man had dare hit me. The previous two slaps came from people who were holding back. Pa and Armand.

When Balthazar slapped me, the stars blurred my vision. I could feel myself falling and then there was darkness.

∾

The man knocked me unconscious…

My eyes fluttered open and I found myself staring at something gold and silky.

And, *my head...*

It had that sensation again. Like it might explode . Not as bad as last time though although it was still pounding.

I blinked several times and moved my head.

Now I was looking at rails. Gold rails. It reminded me of a bird cage.

I shuffled and saw more rails then I made the mistake of bolting up right because now my head felt like it just might fall off.

It would have been the least of my worries because the reason why the rails reminded me of a cage was because I was in a cage.

I was in a fucking cage!

"No…" I cried and brought my hands up to my cheeks.

I was in a cage.

I shook my head as I looked around.

This was a bedroom. There was a massive four poster bed in the center of the room with a large French window leading out what I thought was a balcony.

But this… this was a cage. A human sized cage in the

room. the gold silk was the padding on the floor. the bedding, like what you'd have for an animal.

The room door opened and Balthazar came in carrying a mug. He looked so ordinary with his mug.

He wore a knitted gray jumper , black slacks and had his dark hair slicked back. If not for the scar running down his cheek he really would have looked just like a regular guy. He smiled when he saw me and set his mug down on a little table by the wardrobe.

"Hello pet, you're awake."

Pet…

My soul shivered. My soul quaked and doom filled me. When Pa told me the other week that he'd put me in a cage if I disobeyed him this was what I imagined. Or where they kept dogs at the pound.

"Not talking?" he cajoled.

"Please let me go. Please…" I resulted to begging.

He came over and got to his knees meeting my level and holding on to the rails of the cage.

The way he looked at me, his coal like eyes lightening with desire I almost thought he was going to actually turn into a monster.

"Say that again pet."

"Please let me go. You don't have to do this."

When he closed his eyes and seemed to relish my words I realized he got off on the begging.

"I could listen to you beg all day. Miss Jia." He opened his eyes and his stare hardened up.

My throat went dry when he stood up, opened the cage door and came inside.

I backed away on my hands. I didn't want him to touch me. I didn't want him to come near me.

There was a limit though, a limit to what I could do. My back reached it when I came up against the cage wall. The rails stopped me from going further.

He knelt down and crawled to me, right up to me and hovered over me, resting his hands either side of me.

"You fascinate me Jia Marchesi. You'll definitely make a good toy. So glad you tried to escape. It gave me the idea to bring you up to my room. I hope you last longer than the last girl, and you're not a screamer. No one but me will hear you." He brought his hand to my cheek and moved close to my lips.

I almost died when he pressed his lips to mine.

Tears streamed down my cheeks as he kissed me and I started to shake.

He laughed at me and moved away again settling back on his hands.

"Sweet like honey," he stated moving back. "I can't wait to taste the rest of you. *Later.*

"Please no. I don't want to. Please." It was instinct to

plead and continue to try even when there was no hope.

"You will Jia. You will want to. Trust me if I think anything other than that you'll die quicker." There was something maddening in his stare that reached out to me and terrified me more.

Uncontrollable tears spilled down my cheeks and all he did was laugh.

CHAPTER 16

Xander

"Here. I think this should do the trick," I stated and tapped a few keys on the key pad.

Dorian smiled. "Holy fucking hell Xander. You and I have got to have some kind of play date when this shite is over."

"Man I wouldn't say no to that." I chuckled and couldn't believe I was laughing.

The last few hours had been a much needed distraction. More than anything we were moving, we were actually doing something and if it went to plan we'd truly be ahead of the game.

"Me either. Don't leave me out," Wes chimed in with a warm smile.

"Of course not."

As if I could leave Wes out of anything.

I could imagine the three of us around computers getting up to all kinds of crazy. We were what you called very dangerous technically minded people.

Together that could mean destruction.

Destruction to certain people who wanted to keep things secret and remain unseen.

That was what we'd done here today.

Dorian brought some of his equipment and gadgets to the house. Some of the stuff was again things I'd never seen because he'd made them himself.

We'd tracked the location of where they had Jia in Twin Falls and realized the place wasn't listed on any map. There was just desert land there. To the naked eye.

The place was an underground facility. It spanned the distance of a few acres of land seemed to have all sorts happening there.

I thought it was some sort of headquarters.

The security and surveillance being used was no mere set up. It was all state of the art and stuff I'd never come across. So I did what I usually did whenever I came across anything like that.

I created a virus. It was something I stumbled across by accident in college.

Most hackers could get through firewalls using specific software. I could do that too. That was like child's play to me. But my specialty was reading codes and it didn't take long for me to figure out how the algorithms were written and in cases like this write something to override the system by attacking it.

It was actually simple really, but I shared my secrets with no one, not even Wes. All I did was copy the code and create a flaw in one of the connecting structures. The key was to create the right kind of flaw. Mine was set to duplicate itself on the same connective coding.

The result would be to wreck the system and wreak havoc right under their noses.

I didn't do it very often because it took away from the element of surprise and slipping in and out of somewhere unseen. Plus most places I had to hack didn't use such state of the art tech.

It took me awhile to analyze the system then create the virus. We'd just let it lose and it was starting to work.

Wes started laughing as the firewall just crumbled down. Those fuckers on surveillance wouldn't even know we could see inside.

Fucking assholes.

"Dammmmmmn," Dorian said. He tapped the mouse and moved it over the different rooms in the facility. "We seriously got in. Okay, I'm going to admit your talent definitely exceeds mine."

"Nah, I don't think so. Think it's the same, we're just good at different things," I assured him.

"That's what I tell myself," Wes chuckled.

Everything was as clear as day. The place was huge, huge and where we'd started looking just had people milling about in a large warehouse space with tons of crates. These guys were workers. Ra workers. They were packing the crates with guns.

Fuck.

I was sure those were all illegal arms. All stolen shit.

It was insane. There were so many crates.

"Well the Feds are gonna have a field day with that. Or whoever we contact." I shook my head at the scenery. It was unbelievable that something like that was going on right underground like it was all so normal. Who knew what the plan was for those weapons.

We moved to a different section of the warehouse and saw a lot of vehicles. Trucks, cars, bikes.

There was a ramp that led to a large door that looked like it opened upwards. I imagined that they drove up there from underground.

That wouldn't be the best way in for us.

The best way to find the best way in was to find Jia

first then go from there. The place had so many rooms though.

"This may take a while," Wes stated. He pulled up a chair and sat next to me. Dorian was to my left.

"I hope not. I want us on the move in an hour or so." I cracked my knuckles. It was eight now. It had taken us all day to get all this stuff together and do what we needed to do.

I'd planned for nine as a ball park time, maybe ten to iron out the plan. Leaving then would give us time to get to the facility under the cover of night fall.

I didn't want us rushing in, and I didn't want us to go over the time either. It would take about four hours to get to there as it was situated at the furthest end of Twin Falls. Right there in between Rocky Creek and San Jacinto.

The terrain there wasn't the best and with the facility not listed on the map it meant we'd have to harness our own map reading skills when we got to a certain point. That meant we needed to be clear from now on our entry points.

"There," Dorian pointed to the section of the facility listed as Executive. "Maybe it would skip out a few areas if we looked there."

I tapped on the section and it brought up fifteen rooms on the screen. They were all meeting rooms though.

The section above that was listed by color and called zones. I clicked on the blue zone and that was when the rooms looked more house like.

I would have clicked past a bird cage like structure in a bedroom if not for the sudden movement inside the cage that caught my attention.

Hair of platinum. Bright in the sunlight, *silver* in the moonlight.

It swished and I saw her face and fury roiled within me.

Jia.

She was in a cage?

She was in a fucking cage!

I growled and balled my fists. Rising to my feet I backed away from the screen.

Wes came over to me and tried to calm me but I backed away further shaking my head.

"They have her in a cage!" I growled. "He locked my girl in a fucking cage! Like an animal."

Instantly I remembered Giovanni threatening the same. I very nearly hit him when I heard it. Now look. It didn't if it was some ironic cruel joke the universe had cast my way. Allowing me to see her that way and be so far away I couldn't do shit.

"Xander, calm down please. We need you calm if this is going to work. Come on bro. I know it's hard but try to cool down." He flicked his palms over and pressed down.

I knew I wasn't helping by losing my head. I just hated the helplessness.

I moved back to my seat but Dorian had taken the mouse and started hovering to the other rooms. It was an actual house.

"I think you're going to have to get in somewhere in the basement section of the meeting rooms," Dorian surmised. "Going any other way won't cut it."

He tapped on a section below the meeting rooms that led to some tunnels. It always came to that. It was the best route though. The most practical.

"We can go through there and get across into the house, get her and go back the way we came," I brainstormed.

"That's the easy way." Dorian smirked. "I'm not so sure it will work out so well though. I have a few things that may come in handy. These guys fight dirty don't they?"

"What do you have in mind?"

"Bombs of sorts. Sleep bombs. Just in case you need to clear a path and there's too many people in the way."

"Thanks."

Jack opened the door to the study and came in. He had a heavy scowl on his face.

"We got another visitor," Jack declared with mock sarcasm.

I was the first to get up.

I followed him out to the living room, to where Frankie held a gun at Armand's head and Giovanni looked him over with delight.

"Found him snooping around outside," Frankie chanted in a sing song voice.

I was already, ready to kill. Seeing this prick here on my turf, in my playground was not good for him.

"I was simply looking for the boss." Armand tried to defend himself. He had his hands raised.

"Oh yeah?" Giovanni asked and got up in his face. "Why didn't you just call me?"

"I wasn't sure you'd answer," Armand replied. It was the first that I'd seen the man look so terrified.

If Giovanni had a gun he would have probably ended him. He didn't need to have a gun though to mess him up.

I stepped forward and he looked to me.

"So Armand, we don't have time for shit, so I'm just going to cut to the part where you're a rat," I accused, just launching in for the kill. No time to ask questions. "You are the fucking rat and you've been playing both sides all a long."

"No, I can explain," Armand shook his head.

Giovanni landed a fist in his face.

"You fucker, how I hoped it wasn't you," Giovanni balked. "How I wished it wasn't you, even when I knew it had to be. Look at all I did for you."

I understood where he was coming from. It was the result of being too trusting.

We'd all been guilty of it. In his case I had no sympathy. Giovanni may be here and we may be working together but it was all for Jia. I was doing it for her. I had no allegiance or compassion for him. Things were not okay, or even cordial between us.

And, he could kill Armand for all I cared.

"I never knew it would get this far." Armand tried to defend himself again.

"What are you really doing here?" Giovanni asked.

"He's watching us. He's part of whoever is watching us. He was just too stupid to do it properly." I answered the question and stared Armand down. He looked to me now. "You, I've nearly killed you once before." I pulled my gun and aimed it at him thinking of all he'd done and facilitated.

Even this, as in what was happening. He'd had some hand in it. He was to blame too.

I pulled the trigger back. It would be so easy to let it go. All I needed to do was recall how he tried to force himself on Jia. It was enough in my head to deserve death. This bastard had done so damn much. Too damn much to be allowed to live.

"Please, no. I was approached by Ethan. He needed someone on the inside watching."

"So you thought that should be you?" Giovanni spat.

"No, it wasn't that."

"*Money.* It was money wasn't it?" Giovanni asked the question as if he was innocent when it came to being tempted by money.

"I'm sorry."

"Sorry? And yet you are here," I pointed out.

I stepped closer, getting up in his face too.

Armand looked like he was going to shit himself. his skin turned pale and his eyes bulged with fright. He knew I'd do it. There would be very little to stop me and there was enough hatred in me to end him.

I hated this guy. I truly hated him and all that he stood for. My finger moved away from the trigger readying to let go.

Jack's hand on my shoulder however made me look to him. I hadn't realized that I was shaking.

Jack shook his head.

"Don't. Don't do it," Jack cautioned, his gaze clung to mine.

I grit my teeth and bit down hard. "Jia is being kept in a cage," I stated. While I kept my gaze trained on him, I noticed Giovanni snap his gaze to me. "This guy helped make that happen. Balthazar Kane is keeping Jia in a Cage. That's what he does. He takes the women he likes and keeps them there so he can do whatever he wants to them."

That was what I'd read. It was fucking Ethan that gave me the synopsis. Tales of disgust was more the fitting description of what that was. Balthazar didn't just rape them and be done with it. it was constant, until they begged for death and even then he would continue and kill them after in the worse possible ways. That was who we were up against. Armand here who was just as bad in my eyes deserved death.

"Xander. It's not our way. It's not worth it. Don't do it boy. I can see the resentment you have for this man. It's not worth it. His blood on your hands is not worth it. let me deal with him." Jack promised. "I'll deal with him in the manner he deserves. Save your energy and strength for what you have ahead. You need a clear mind when dealing with people like Balthazar, and remember its' not just him. You have the Spades and Ethan. Ra people. This guy isn't worth it."

If it was anyone else besides Jack, they might not have been able to reach me. To reach inside me to the person I was and speak to that guy. I hadn't been him in so long I forgot what it was like.

It wasn't our way to kill the way I was going to kill Armand. If I killed him now I knew it would be on my mind. I squinted and pulled in a ragged breath then lowered the gun and walked out of the room.

I went outside for some air. I needed it. I just needed to clear my head so I could focus.

Patience wasn't one of my strong points at all.

I hated having to be patient and I hated having to wait or have obstacles in my fucking way.

Jack followed me out. I looked to him and instantly felt ashamed for the way I was going to kill Armand. Although he would have deserved it.

"You cool?" he asked me.

"I'm trying. I'm trying. Jack I just need to get her back."

"We're working on it. *You* are working on it."

I nodded. Then I thought of Balthazar.

"Jack, when I see Balthazar, he's dead. I won't show the same compassion I just showed Armand." I just had to let him know.

He agreed. "Son, nobody would stop you from killing that motherfucker. Definitely not me. He killed Claire."

I drew in a deep breath and moved to go back inside. I had to finish up this plan and get it on the move.

Balthazar's blood was calling to me.

CHAPTER 17

Xander

WE LEFT at nine like I hoped, in a party of two trucks.

Two teams.

One would stay on the outside. The rest was going in for the rescue.

One truck had ten marine recons Jack had commissioned for this black op mission.

He'd gotten the best. Guys would were the best in what they did. We had three snipers, two gunners and the rest were front men. Jack gave them their own specific orders.

My truck carried me, Jack, Giovanni, Frankie and

four marines who were going in with us. Wes and
Dorian stayed behind as planned to be my eyes.

It was a good team. There were some seriously
skilled men here. All put together I would say we had a
chance.

I just hated it. All of it.

It all reminded me of the last time. It was too much
of a reminder of what happened last time. My thoughts
were consumed with the memory for the whole journey. The whole time I went over everything that had
happened.

It was most likely down to the fact that last time was
when I actually had a battle with the Ra.

I never even got close to Balthazar.

All I did was see him kill Claire and throw the
grenade that took me out.

That was it, and previously I never got close either.
Not close enough to land a fist in his face, get a good
shot, or anything like that.

Of all those times —and they were really terrible
times —this felt like the worst.

All those other times he'd never had anyone close to
me from the beginning. It was always a surprise attack
that knocked me for six.

The first memorable time was when he
kidnapped Vlad Hanflick and blew up the orphanage.
The next that stood out was of course when he lured

my team in by taking one of our own and killed everyone.

This time I'd already experienced the damage. He'd taken Jia and I didn't know what he could be doing to her or what he could have done.

Frankie nudged me in my side and I looked to him.

I was sitting away from everyone. Closer to the driver. I'd done that on purpose so I could think. Frankie however took it as an invite to sit near me.

Jack was at the far end of the truck going over some stuff with the marines and Giovanni sat by himself.

"I don't like the quiet," Frankie stated. "Not when shit's going down."

I glanced at him. I preferred quiet especially in those times. I also wasn't the best person to talk to.

"Sometimes it's good to reflect," I answered hoping he'd take the hint that I didn't want to talk.

He didn't. I suspected that was on purpose too.

"Sometimes you do too much reflecting. See that's the difference between mafia guys and the others. We talk it out and act as a unit. That's us. We know what's on the other guys mind so we have his back before he can even ask."

"I'm not like that. And…" my voice trailed off as I glanced over at Giovanni who was just staring over at the wall. In his casual wear he looked so different from what I was used to. His presence was making me worse.

I had the prints in my backpack. I'd keep them close to me.

Frankie followed my gaze and shook his head. When he looked back to me he sighed.

"Kid, I get it," he said with an uneasy smile. "I do, but right now we're in this together. We're going in for the same goal, same cause. I've been watching over Jia since she was a little girl. It gets to me too that this has happened. It's why I'm here. We just have to work together."

"Yeah. I'm grateful you're here Frankie. We wouldn't have made it this far. I'd be dead and I wouldn't get the chance to help in some way. Whatever that way is." I'd fully accepted that I was by no means out of the woods yet. Not by a long shot. I wouldn't be either until this was truly over and Balthazar dead, dead, dead.

I'd always be looking for him. Always seeking vengeance. Until I got it.

"This Balthazar guys seems to be of the worst variety. Shoot on sight?" he asked.

I nodded. "Shoot on fucking sight pal. No questions to ask." There was nothing. Nothing I needed to know. I got the answers I'd wanted from the past and found out the link was Ethan. The traitor was him. He was the link that connected everything. What else did I need to know?

"Then I'll aim for his head when I see him."

That was exactly the plan I had too.

You couldn't negotiate with people like Balthazar. You just had to take them down.

I'd aim for his head and blow it off his miserable body.

We got to the clearing a little earlier than planned.

Earlier was better.

We got set up outside some caves on the other side of where we wanted to be. The landscape around was a mixture of mountain range, desert and groves of trees here and there. In the bright daylight the place would look similar to being around certain parts of the Grand Canyon minus the green.

We were aiming for the route Dorian suggested which was through the meeting rooms and office section of the facility.

Although we were going in as one, I'd split the guys going inside into two further teams for the purposes of getting direction from Wes and Dorian.

Jack was in charge of the marine guys and they would get direction from Dorian. I was in charge of Giovanni and Frankie. I got Wes. I needed Wes for more reasons than just direction.

My best friend sometimes had a way of helping me to focus, just from hearing his voice.

Once we'd gathered the things we needed we were ready. We then gathered together in a circle by the trucks and I stood at the head to give the last piece of guidance.

"Guys this is a very dangerous mission," I began. "The people we're going to see are known terrorists and they won't care about protecting themselves. Their goal if they see us will be to stop us and that means sacrificing themselves to do that. The Spades in the Ra are the elite. They are skilled. Very skilled. If you get in the vicinity of any of them shoot to kill."

I thought that was the best advice I could give anyone. The shoot to kill missions were always the most difficult because often times you weren't given the full run down of the crimes that made it so. You just had to shoot to kill and it felt more assassin like. I didn't really like those sorts, but there was always a very good reason behind them.

Everyone nodded and looked ready.

I noticed how quiet Giovanni was. It was unnerving. I wasn't used to it.

That fucking asshole was always blowing up about something, or shooting his mouth of about shit.

I took the lead and led everyone down the path. It was dark. Pitch black at one a.m. Perfect though for what we needed. I hoped we could be out of here by sunrise.

There was a cave that led to the tunnels. Dorian told us we could get to the entrance that way so we went through there. Next was the one mile walk to the entrance to the facility.

It reminded me a lot of the secret chamber Giovanni had.

Had that same shit smell too that made me want to heave. The facility was supposed to be hidden but I was certain anyone who happened upon the place would know from the smell that people were here somewhere.

We got to the entrance and the guys took out their tools to get in. The best part of the virus I set up for the place was that we could hack the rest of the system.

I got Dorian to replay the last couple of hours of footage so nobody would be any wiser on our entry. Nobody would know we were here.

Not one iota.

We got inside a section that looked like a large storage room.

"Here's where you guys gotta be careful," Wes spoke into my ear piece. His voice was as clear as if he was right next to me. "There's a few patrol guards walking the floors just outside. Everything else is quiet."

"Is there a path we can take that will evade him?" I asked.

"When you go outside head up the corridor then take a sharp right. Go down the stairs and follow the path on the map."

That sounded like a good plan. Wes had made us maps that would definitely come in handy. He'd done a straightforward route to Jia and another with details of the whole place.

"Thanks Wes." I looked to Jack and the others. "Just follow me guys. There's a guard outside so let's get in stealth mode."

When they nodded I turned to continue to where Wes directed. We got out seamlessly and I almost felt hopeful that this would work. We'd gotten into this facility. This secret facility we'd christened Ra head-quarters.

That had to be a plus for us. Something to hang on to.

We got down the path where Wes directed and the next thing to do was go up. we had to go up and the best way up was by using the stairs. The problem with the stairs though was the chance that other people could be using it too.

I led the guys out to the stairwell. It was one hell of a size for back stairs. There was an elevator shaft next to it. We needed to get to the tenth floor.

We proceeded up as quickly as we could go but

something caught my attention just as we got to the fifth floor. It was a little light that flickered.

"Stop." I held my hand up and the guys all stopped.

The light came back and grew bigger as it flickered over us. Then it split into two as it bounced over us, then five.

Fuck!

I realized in an instant that it must have been some type of motion detector that had been manually set up in the security system. Something that didn't go down when I scrambled the security.

Shit!

The lights all jumped together and started swirling into a vicious circle. There was a snapping sound by the doors like they were sealing shut. Right from the bottom where we'd come and up.

"Guys move. Run! Get to the next floor and get out." I called out, but fuck, the light turned into some laser beam and cut right through two of the marines with Jack. Without warning their bodies cut in half before us and fell to the ground. They were dead before they even realized they were.

When we saw that I didn't need to give any further command. We all ran and tried to avoid the lasers that were growing bigger and gaining on us.

We got to the next floor but the doors wouldn't open.

This looked like the atrium and there were three separate door entrances.

Jack rushed across to the door nearest him and opened it. We followed but by the time we got there the laser lights were there. The only escape for me and Giovanni was to rush to the other door.

We only fucking got through by the skin of our teeth.

I looked through the glass panel in the door and saw the laser lights swirling in a mass of bright light. There was no way that any of us could go back that way.

No way in hell.

And now we were all split up.

"Jack can you hear me?" I said into my communicator.

"Yeah. We're good Xander. Let's just keep going. Whoever gets to Jia first grabs her. See you outside boy."

I really hoped so. I really did.

I looked to Giovanni and he frowned.

The two of us stuck together just sucked the hope away from me.

CHAPTER 18

Jia

WHEN PA LOCKED me away in my room when I was sixteen I thought it was the worst thing in the world.

My little room had an ensuite bathroom so it was easy to keep me in there without letting me out. I got food given to me five times a day. Whatever I asked for.

In the beginning I was so distraught over ma's death that I didn't really get frustrated about being locked away.

It made sense that Pa wanted to keep me safe. After all I'd been seconds away from death and he'd saved me.

That was what happened. So I never said anything when he told me to stay in my room and stationed a guard by the door.

I felt safe.

Unlike the cage I was in, my room looked more similar to a fancy penthouse suite in a hotel with all the stuff I'd loved as a teenager.

I never had posters of boys I liked or bands.

I was different and loved the medieval look. I had a four poster wrought iron bed with the chandelier to match and instead of lightbulbs I loved candles. I had floor boards with various candlesticks decorating the place.

It was beautiful and looked like it had been pulled from a painting.

The first few weeks of being locked up weren't back but the next few were awful and Pa got aggressive as he looked for the men who'd assisted in breaking into our home. He was out for the blood of everybody. Not just the man who'd been responsible for the damage.

I'd heard gun shots a lot when people pissed him off and soon the whole being locked away in my room thing came to light for what it truly was.

It was somewhere I loved but I was a prisoner in my own home. Not allowed to leave, not allowed to speak to anyone.

It was safety.

Not like this.

I was scared to sleep, because earlier when I dosed off I woke up to find Balthazar watching me and touching himself.

As if he hadn't creeped the fuck out of me enough.

As if I hadn't had enough of the disgusting creeps that had come my way, it seemed like my end would come with the worst of them all. This asshole.

It had to be late now. Very late and the room was lit by a lamp.

I sat in the cage waiting.

It was a while ago since I'd seen him but what I wanted to see was him come in and go to bed.

The plan was very simple, quite unlike the plan to escape that had gone to hell earlier.

It was simply this: once he came in and went to sleep I'd sleep too. I'd close my eyes and sleep.

Of course that was providing his promise of having *later* didn't mean now, or anytime soon.

He looked like one of those guys, those creeps who liked the game. Who liked the fear. That was what I'd worked out.

I remembered Anya watching one of her criminal mind shows. She loved anything like that. While I'd complained because I didn't want to miss the start of the Real Housewives of Beverly hills, she'd been glued to the screen watching a show about serial killers. It was supposed to be our girls night in.

The girl had a good head on her keeping up to date and clued up on things like that. Maybe if I wasn't raised around so much guns and violence I too would have delved into those sorts of shows. What I loved though was more of an escape for me.

If however, I'd watched a little more of criminal minds with Anya I may be able to figure this guy out more than I had.

What I did guess though was that fear was a big turn on. The more afraid I got the more turned on he got. Only time could procure the fear because the longer I stayed in here the worse I got. Add the ways he'd both grossed me out and creeped me out to the mixture and I was one damn mess that would be perfect for him.

Footsteps sounded outside the door.

My heart squeezed at first and was so painful in my chest I thought I was going to have a heart attack. I could barely breathe, could barely take my next breath.

Jesus...

The door opened and I sucked in a few short breaths to keep from passing out and also to steady my fear.

He came in and closed the door behind him.

I was really hoping and praying he'd just go over to his bed and sleep, or go change in the bathroom and

QUEEN OF HIS HEART

then come to bed, but he looked like he had other things on his mind.

His gaze instantly snapped to me in a feral, primal way. It reminded me of some sort of savage beast who'd just picked up the scent of their prey.

Savage, that was him to a T.

He kept his gaze trained on me sitting in the cage with my knees hugged to my chest.

He backed off his jacket, tossed it on the chair nearby and came over to me.

When he opened the cage door tears stung the backs of my eyes.

This was it. God... this was it.

I didn't know what the hell I was supposed to do now.

What the hell could I do to stop him from doing whatever he wanted to me?

He kept standing this time instead of coming down to me.

"Still awake," he chanted in a sing song taunting voice. "Still wide awake. She thinks it's better to stay awake so she can see what happens next. That's okay, should have gotten your rest though. You needed it."

"I'm not tired," I replied. It was a lie and we both knew it was.

Exhaustion had come for me hours ago and I was certain if I felt the way I did –like I hadn't slept in forever – then I must have looked exactly like that too. I was sure.

He answered with a smile. "You know it's amazing when you aim for something and end up killing two birds with one stone. You were Plan B, although you were my plan A. It's so much simpler to just hit where it hurts. Go to the weakness. It never fails. I'd planned to take you from the get go and make your father give me those damn blueprints. If I had everything would be over, I'd be richer, you'd be dead already, him too for being so annoying as fuck. But guess what?" he laughed a crude sardonic laugh that made my skin crawl. "I like it this way. Ethan wanted to do things as clean cut as possible. No kidnapping and no unnecessary deaths. I'm so glad I listened to him. Had I not, I wouldn't have known how much Xander Cage cared for you. I wouldn't have known it one bit. I would never have known that the man was still alive and looking for me. I didn't know how that managed to slip under the net. He's good like that though. Better than me, but that might be because I like a cameo every now and again. It shakes people up and they know I'm not some myth. I'm their worst nightmare."

"Do you just like to hear the sound of your voice." I had to ask because I didn't know why he thought I needed some content to what had happened. Right now I just wanted to die.

He laughed again. "Just like your father. You really are a Marchesi. I like my women fiery. The point of my speech that seems to have bored you was to tell you I'm glad I'll get to take another woman Xander holds so dear to his heart. I never got to have fun with the first one. I'd planned to cut her head off and send it to him, but she wouldn't have allowed herself to get caught the way you did. And fear was lost on her. Nothing scared that woman. Your fear arouses me."

And his words sickened me.

Of course I would have to be the one to be weak. Unlike Claire as he quite rightly pointed out.

I didn't answer although he gave me an expectant glare like he was expecting me to give an answer.

"Stand up," he demanded.

I stood on shaky legs.

No point protesting or fighting simple commands.

"Take your clothes off." He spoke so cool and calm as if he was talking about the weather.

"No, please." I shook my head. "Please, please."

He smiled and pulled a gun from his back pocket. He pointed it at me and my whole body seized up with numbness.

"Take your clothes off... *now*! Or I'll shoot you. Handing you over to your father alive is a courtesy. But push me and I may change my mind."

I started to shake and tremble knowing he meant

every word. He'd do it. This man was some kind of monster. He'd have no compassion. He didn't care.

When he pulled the trigger back I slipped the straps of my dress down and pushed it down the length of my body so I could step out of it.

Fuck...

I was doing this. I was taking off my clothes in front of this mad man. I couldn't even drag it out because I didn't have much to take off.

Just the dress and my underwear. My underwear which was next but I went for my sandals instead.

"No, no, nice try. Leave those on." He waved the gun down at my feet and beckoned me to straighten up. "Bra and panties off now."

I looked at him and stared long and hard deciding I couldn't do it.

I couldn't.

I lowered and instead of dragging down my panties like he thought I would do I pulled my dress back on.

I was done. If this was it then this was it. He may think I was weak and defenseless but that didn't mean I had to be.

I shocked him to shit when I stepped forward, right in the line of the gun.

"Kill me. Just kill me. If that's an option I want that." I squared off with him. "You won't treat me like shit and make me take my clothes off so you can fuck me before you kill me. Kill me first."

It was the most bravest thing I'd ever done in my life and he didn't like it.

He growled and raised his hand to slap me again but a knock sounded at the door.

He looked to it eyes blazing and stormed out of the cage.

"Come in," he called out.

A dark haired guy as tall as him came in carrying a machine gun. "We have company boss. Giovanni and Cage are here and they brought company. They also screwed with the surveillance."

Xander and Pa was here?

Together?

They were really here?

Oh God… my heart started beating again. It felt like it had stopped and started up when hope sparked from deep within.

Balthazar bared his teeth like the animal he was, picked up the little vase that was on the table, and launched it across the room.

"Fuckkkkk!!!! What the fuck are you saying to me?" Balthazar bellowed.

"What should we do?" the guy asked.

Balthazar looked to me, marched over and grabbed

my arm so hard it popped and I almost thought he was going to pull it out of its socket.

He yanked me and pulled me out of the room. The guy followed behind.

"They crossed me." Balthazar scuffed as we walked down the corridor. "That's fine. I'll shit all over them. They really have another thing coming if they think they can just come in here on some crazy rescue mission. Get Ethan."

"Yes boss," the man said and diverted down the path in the opposite direction.

Balthazar snapped is gaze to me and scowled deep. "This just got more interesting, sugar. It sure did. But good for you, you get to watch your boyfriend and your father die."

"No!" I cried trying to shake him off me.

"Yes, yes, yes." He sang loud on top of his voice.

He dragged me to a control room where there was several TV screens. A guard sat in front of them.

The eight screens that were in a row all had the same thing. It was footage of some offices. There was one screen however that had something different.

When Xander and Pa came into view I sucked in a sharp breath.

Balthazar saw my reaction and laughed.

"Wonderful, I'm gonna enjoy this. Let's spice it up

with some fun. Release the poison gas," Balthazar ordered. "We can start with that and see who dies first."

I looked to the screen wishing I could warn them.

Instead I was going to watch then die.

They came for me.

They came…

CHAPTER 19

Xander

"CAN I at least have a fucking gun?" Giovanni snapped, glaring at me as he stopped in his tracks.

We'd been walking down a dark corridor. It was off route to where we'd originally wanted to go, but now our new route.

I stopped too and returned the seething look he was giving me.

It was understandable as fuck why I wouldn't trust him with any kind of weapon around me. Realistically though, he did actually need to protect himself, given what just happened.

Frowning, I pulled out a long reach knife and held it out to him. At least, if he got any bright ideas and went rogue on me I'd be able to handle him better with a knife than a gun.

"Are you fucking kidding me?" he barked and glared at me.

"Take it or leave it pal, you're the one who fucking tortured me." I wasn't about to just forget that, not for a second. "Want me to trust you with a gun?"

He bared his teeth like a wild animal and took the knife. He looked it over with disdain and shook his head.

Ignoring him, I started walking again and he caught up.

As we'd proceeded down the path some little lights came on. It was all very ominous and tension grew with every step I took. I'd been waiting for something more to happen and nothing had. It was ten minutes ago that we'd gotten separated from the others and three of our marines killed. Just like that.

What else was going to happen?

"It's too quiet," Giovanni observed.

I couldn't even give him the cold front of silence I'd been sporting since he'd come on the scene. He was right.

"I know," I agreed.

He stopped again and looked around. "Something's

wrong. Something doesn't feel right. It's like we're going and it feels like a damn trap. They must know we're here."

I gazed at him. maybe the tension was screwing with my abilities. Yes I could sense that something was off and agreed that they must have known something was wrong, but I didn't get the sensation of the trap.

"What are you thinking?" I asked him.

"This is the trap, where's the bait? We're in the mouth of hell, where are the demons? Even with your … whatever it was you did with the security and surveillance cameras someone would have checked out the stair well and seen the dead marines. But there's no one looking around. Nobody checking things out."

As he spoke it dawned on me why that could be. Why it was that nobody might be checking things out.

"They can see us," I breathed. A jolt of panic rushed through my body.

He nodded. "I believe so and we're heading to God knows."

I tapped my wire to speak to Wes. "Wes are you there? Can you see what's up ahead?"

I narrowed my eyes when there was no answer.

Giovanni widened his.

I looked at the wire clipped to my collar and checked the connection. It seemed fine.

"Wes, come in Wes. Come in."

"EMP. They've sent some kind of electromagnetic pulse to fry the connection." Giovanni growled. "I use something similar when I suspect undercover cops and feds at the Marchesi."

"*Fuck.*"

"Yes, we are fucked. What the hell are we supposed to do now?"

My God, we were fucked.

I closed my eyes and thought. This required raw skill. It required raw balls to the wall skill and it meant I had to focus above the fucking rim. It meant I had to push Jia out of my mind and get the damn job done.

Giovanni rested a heavy hand on my shoulder and my eyes snapped open.

He moved his hand away but continued to stare at me.

"All things aside ... if none of this shit had happened, I would have chosen you for her. It means nothing for me to say that to you now, and I still would have killed you because that's who I am, but if none of this had happened and I was thinking straight things would have turned out different. This was what I feared and when it comes to my daughter I can't think straight." He pulled in a haggard breath. "When my wife was killed Jia was seconds away from death too, that stayed in my mind. It stayed there and I never forgot that a few seconds could have taken her from me. It was what I had in the forefront of my mind when shit hit the fucking fan with the Ra. It's why I treated you the way I did."

All I could do was stare at him. I didn't know what he expected me to say to any of that. I understood it, but I wasn't about to brush all that happened under the rug.

"What's the point of telling me this now?"

"It's not an apology Xander. I'm not saying sorry because if I had another chance I would do the same thing. All over again. What it is, is an explanation. And it's to let you know that Jia needs you. You must have been damn good at whatever it is you do for the Ra to get you to steal from me. Maybe you need to be that person now."

I agreed wholeheartedly with that.

Fuck... I absolutely had to be that person.

"Yeah," I answered and I had a really bad idea. "I need you to cover me. I need you to be you too."

"Well Ace, I'm gonna need something a little better than this." He held up the knife.

I handed him a Berretta and he smiled.

"Better?" I asked.

"Much." He positioned it.

"Let's go."

We started walking again and that was when I saw a

mist ahead. Instinct made me stop. I'd seen that before on one of my missions in the Middle East.

It was absolute confirmation that they could fucking see us, because since when did the inside corridor that separated meeting rooms mist up like we were in the middle of the forest on a dark night?

"Back this way," I shouted. "It's poison. We have to go up."

As in up on the next level up.

Giovanni was on the move. I was surprised how fast he could run.

Those motherfuckers really knew how to drop shit.

Fuck.

We ran back the way we came looking for a way up .

There was nowhere. The only other way was to keep going until we got to the stair well and that was a big no. There was no elevator nearby either.

And fucking hell the damn mist of shit was starting to pour out now like someone turned it up. Going in one of the rooms we passed wasn't even an option. That was perhaps what they wanted us to do, then get marooned inside unable to do anything about it then die like vermin or the pests they thought we were.

Fucking bastards.

Fuck them.

Giovanni stood back and started shooting at the

ceiling. When it gave, I started shooting up too in the same spot. The only way was up.

Up.

A small crack formed and Giovanni stepped back lacing his fingers together so I could step on to his hands.

"You're lighter, move quickly," he bellowed.

I didn't argue. I was lighter than him and more agile. I moved, hoisting myself up to the ceiling by stepping on to his hands. I tore away at the plaster in the ceiling , coming in contact with all the wooden beams. Latching on to one I grabbed on to it and pulled myself up, then rebounded to lower down and reach for him.

The mist was just nearing him now. a few seconds and it would surround him.

He looked to it as if contemplating to stay. Then I realized he actually was.

"Go, get her and get out of here," he cried looking back to me.

"Giovanni, don't you fucking tell me shit like that. Get here now," I balked talking to him like we were out on the battlefield and he was in my command.

When the mist started surrounding his legs that was when the bastard decided to reach up.

I was still weak from his torture but I homed in on all my strength and pulled him up. Once he got to a height he grabbed on to the wooden beam too and lifted himself the rest of the way.

We both moved away from the mist as it started rising and ran to a safer distance away from it. The floor we were on was similar to the one we'd just come from but had wider corridors.

I glanced across at Giovanni and noted the stern expression on his face.

He was serious back there. He got me first and would have stayed there and died. He may have been one evil bastard but when it came to Jia no one had to guess that the man would do anything for his daughter.

Anything, anything at all.

"Xander," Giovanni called out when we turned the next corner. He grabbed my arm, pulling me to a stop.

"What? We have to keep moving," I urged.

The wildness in his eyes got to me. "If I don't make it out of here, and you get to her, you take care of her. Just make sure she's safe. That's all I'm asking. You don't owe me anything, but you love her so I'm asking to just make sure she's safe." His eyes pleaded with mine. It felt like and extension of his previous talk. But with more heart since he nearly did just die.

I leaned in close and wrenched my arm free of his grasp.

"You know I will," I told him.

"Thank you."

I nearly told him he didn't have to thank me but I let it go. I humored him because I knew what it meant to him to have my word. It was just like when I started working for him. He'd told me Jia was the most important thing to him and if anything happened I was to protect her.

We continued out to the atrium an there we were greeted by the company we were expecting.

At a glance I counted about fifty men all armed and ready to end us.

Yes, it had been quiet.

Now it was time to make noise.

CHAPTER 20

Xander

Bullets started flying.

They didn't give us any warning.

Why the fuck would they?

I pulled my two Berettas and started firing forward.

Just like I asked Giovanni had my back.

As the first bullet came our way he slipped behind me and we were back to back, shooting at the men that surrounded us as if we planned it that way.

"Yes, come for me you fuckers. This is how we deal with pests in Italy," Giovanni cried.

I just heard bullets then a thump. I was too occupied

with the guys in front of me who were shooting. To shoot like this it required precision and tact to make sure you didn't get hit. And, with bullets flying from everywhere it was near impossible.

Near, but not.

"I'm moving forward, take care of the guys behind," I called to Giovanni.

Cool as it was that we were so synced, we couldn't stay like that. There were too many of them.

He ran behind and did as I said. That left me to deal with the men in front.

Someone, however, slammed into me from the side. Came out of nowhere, knocked into me hard and I crashed into the barrier that led over the balcony. The impact made me drop my guns and it fucking felt like I'd broken another rib.

Shit.

I fell to the ground and whirled around to see a goliath sized guy balling his fists to land both into me.

I tried to dodge the blow but couldn't move fast enough. That hit I'd taken to my chest in the barrier really took it out of me.

Fuck, as his massive fists pounded into me I saw stars then blackness. I had to will myself not to black out. I didn't even know that was humanly possible but I did it. I couldn't fuck this up.

Jia needed me. If I got captured we'd all be dead. It wouldn't just be her. It would be all of us.

The guy went for my bag and I realized he must have known the prints were inside. I flicked myself up and roared through the pain that took me, along with the strength, channeling both to fuel me as I propelled myself forward and knocked him to the ground.

He pulled a gun on me and tried to shoot my head off when he pulled the trigger back.

I'd learned long ago though that with these types of people you had to fight dirty. It was my intention when I pulled my long reach knife from its sheath and gouged his eyes out, then stabbed him to the heart.

I spared no time to check if he was dead. I grabbed my guns again and moved forward looking around for Giovanni but I couldn't see him anywhere.

I shoot three guys who came at me from the upper level and continued running down the corridor then through the double doors.

Shit there were more guys.

I raised my guns and fired shot after shot taking down as many as I could, but there were too many and now I didn't have anyone else to back me up.

A group of guys rushed me even though I was shooting. Two went down but the rest got through.

I gave one a round house kick and swooped into a side

sweep kick that took out another. Jumping into the air I sent a flying kick down another guy's throat and fired another three shots at three guys blowing their heads off.

I tucked and rolled only to be faced with more guys coming from the end of the corridor to my left.

Fuck.

There were so many.

Just now took the life out of me. This was wasting my God damn time.

Shit.

I stood up and aimed getting ready to fire again, but they started dropping dead.

Bullets whizzed down from above and I looked around to see Jack, Frankie , the remaining marines that came in with us and five of the marines we'd left outside with rifles.

They had my back.

My whole body sighed with relief.

"Boy, head down the corridor, quick, that bastard has her over some pit," Jack yelled pointing down the path to my right. He started running too heading down to where I was.

I ran down the path and through another set of double doors. This part looked entirely different. It was more like the factory style set up I'd gone to in Nepal. The place were Claire died. This area looked like that.

I was going full speed ahead until a shot hit the metal piping hovering over me.

I stopped and snapped around to see Ethan coming at me with a shot gun.

Good, it was time to start seeing some of the people I'd wanted to kill the fuck dead the most.

Like an animal I launched myself at the asshole. He thought he was a match for me with that gun.

He was not. But maybe he would be with the machine gun he'd started to use.

I had to jump out of the way to avoid being hit and scuttle over to hide behind another set of pipes. These were large and tubular, almost big enough for me to fit inside.

"Yes, you think you can get me!" He taunted jeering me. "Give me the fucking prints Xander. Give them the fuck to me!"

"Go fuck yourself you fucking dog!" I cried back. Word attack, word vomit, whatever anyone wanted to call it, it was just a taste of all I'd wanted to say. There was so much to say to him, yet none of it really mattered.

The result of being betrayed was feeling betrayed.

The emotion coiled through my whole body, being this close to him. Within the vicinity of him.

I wasn't close enough though. Not to do the damage I wanted.

The aim was just to get to him. If I could get close I could get him.

I *would* be able to get him and take him down.

I rolled over as he came at me and decided to just go for him using one of my crazy tactics. People innately assumes you'd retreat from danger, not go toward it.

It was built in us to flee at the sign of anything that could kill us.

I flipped that around every time as a surprise attack. This time it worked no less than it always had.

I went straight to him and stunned him. I managed to knock him to the ground even as he fired the shots. He dropped the gun and the two of us rolled over a couple of times from the impact of my attack.

He moved before me to try and get me but I didn't allow it. I got him first with all the rage inside me.

I'd been building for him and Balthazar.

I'd been building up and ready for them.

I pounded into his face knocking off his eye patch revealing the sealed skin of what used to be his right eye. He'd never told me how he lost it. No matter, he was about to lose the left.

This prick had done so much damage to me. Damage of trust, damage of everything. Made me go against my internal warnings of trusting people and I ended up trusting him out of friendship.

Bastard!

I hit him again in his face and as he howled with pain I really thought I had him. Except a jab to my side right in the fucking rib that was broken made me double over and lose my edge. I lost my momentum and he gained the upper hand.

He flipped me off him and was ready to pulled his hand gun when blood splattered through his shoulder and splashed all over my face.

Fuck!

Another bullet pierced his side and he dropped to the ground.

I shuffled away from Ethan's flapping arms as Jack rushed over to us and sent a kick to his head snapping it backwards, knocking him to the ground.

I jumped to my feet and joined him.

Jack held the gun down at Ethan who was spurting blood and bleeding out. He lifted his head to look at the both of us.

"Xander go rescue your girl. I have to talk to this dog about Claire," Jack said to me.

As I looked at him I was so glad he'd come with me. This was his fight too. He'd been friends with Ethan for years before he'd known me.

It was right that he got to finish this with him.

My fight was with Balthazar Kane.

I nodded and ran to leave them.

With each step I knew that what I'd just gone

through was just the prep. I hadn't gotten the big boss yet. I hadn't gotten to the big boss in this game.

I was on my way to him, running and gathering strength. Blocking out the pain in my side.

Jack had said that Jia was over some pit. It didn't sound good when he'd said it and looking around where I was I knew there was no part of this that I was going to like. Not one damn bit whatsoever.

It would be all fucked up just like Balthazar. That was his style.

Bizarre and outrageous.

I reached another set of double doors. It was the only place left for me to go.

The only path left to follow.

I went in and cursed myself when I saw just how damn right I was.

I experienced what I could only express as a gamut and tumult of clashing emotions.

My heart had lifted at the sight of Jia ahead of me, then in the same second, everything crushed inside when I saw what that evil bastard had done to her.

Jia was gagged and tied to a pole.

This was some sort of refinery room or hall. The place was massive and yes there was a fucking pit.

The pole Jia was tied to was attached to a platform and it hovered over the pit.

There were two suspension bridges that led to where she was.

It looked like there was water below her because I saw a splash of it.

I held my gun up getting ready and moved out, closer, closer then I stopped as shock number two presented itself.

Yes, the pit was full of water.

And crocodiles!

Fucking crocodiles.

It looked like a seen from some kind of horror movie.

Jia cried and made a muffled scream as the platform she was on lowered by a few inches.

My God... it was remote controlled.

And who was controlling the remote?

Balthazar stepped out from my left and held up the remote.

He smiled at me like we were old friends who hadn't seen each other in years.

"Xander, wow. So good to see you," he bubbled.

"Wish I could say the same about you," I yelled. "Actually, I don't wish that. Not one fucking bit. You mother fucking dog. You fucking prick of an asshole. Let her go. Let her go right the fuck now."

He laughed and pretended to shiver. "Ohhhhh

awwwwww I'm so scared. Big Bad Xander's come to get me. Wowwwwwwwww."

The prick of an asshole knew how to get me worked up the fucking wrong way.

"Don't fuck with me."

"No, I know not to do that. The thing about you though my good man is this… you wear your heart on your sleeve for all to see your damn weakness." He waved the remote over to Jia, pressed it and the platform lowered an inch more. The crocs swam closer to her and she let out another muffled scream.

"Nooooo!" I shouted. "Fuck you. No!!!"

"Put the gun down," he said in a cool voice that carried an edge of sharpness.

I set the gun down. I had no choice. If he pressed that damn remote one more time one of the crocs would get to her. They'd be able to climb up on the platform.

I couldn't let that happen.

"So, here's the four one, one. You give me the blueprints."

"I give you the prints and you let her go," I demanded.

He shook his head. "I don't think so." He glanced down at his watch. "By my records of time you people shouldn't even be here so that deal is out the window. It's null and void, no negotiation where she is released to you. However..." He held up his hands and the smile on his horrible face widened. "I will allow you to decide how she dies and the rate too. I was trying to work out which was best. Method, or rate of acceleration. So I decided on both."

"You evil prick, just let her go. I'm here with the fucking prints." At this point I didn't care about the blueprints. I'd already calculated in my head that I needed to save Jia and to do that I'd have to give him what he wanted.

"Yes, you are here with the prints. The prints that I still need to check but that's not really the point. I don't work like that. I don't like you Xander Cage. I don't think that's a secret. I was furious to hear you were still alive but saw you as an advantage to play nice with Ethan. Play nice with Ethan and get the prints nice and smooth. Then you fucked up and we ended up wasting so much damn time when we could have played dirty in the first place by taking the girl. You need to pay for that. so this is it. So, tell me how should I kill her? A bullet to the hell like your previous lady love, or should I just release the control and give her a good dip in the croc pool?" He laughed.

I bit down hard on my back teeth and stared at him.

He was sick. Sick and deranged. That is what came to my mind as I listened to him.

"You sick fuck. Give her to me or you don't get shit!" I roared.

One more press of the remote and Jia's platform lowered.

"Xander Cage, you are not in a position to be making demands." He smiled and the asshole shot down the ropes holding the suspension bridge nearest us. As the bridge crashed into the water the crocs went crazy.

The worst part of that was that was my route to her. That was the way to get to her. The other bridge was connected to the other side of the fucking room. I would have had to go out and find the entrance to get there.

I glanced at her, tears glistened her cheeks and her eyes pools of water.

I remembered when I first saw her. The image Ethan had shown me. Not the sight of her in the club. The image.

What I saw in her eyes was desperation. It called to me. It had called to me then and it screamed to me now.

It bellowed and here I was just looking at her. Just watching her.

Unable to help.

Just like Claire.

"Awwww, you should see your face," Balthazar taunted. I returned my focus to him. "You really

QUEEN OF HIS HEART

should Xander Cage. You're a pitiful mess. But don't worry this time when I kill you, I'll make sure you're dead."

I narrowed my gaze at him, and thought long and hard.

Fuck...

Think... I needed to get out of this mess. I needed to save Jia.

How though?

"Come on Xander don't fight this? Give me the prints."

"No." I shook my head. "Her first. Give her to me."

I was going to try something. Every time I pissed him off he lowered the remote. If I could get it from him or away from him she'd be okay.

I just needed to get it away from him.

This time he made a show of holding it out. He got ready to press that damn button but a bullet sizzled through his arm.

He dropped the remote and yelped. A quick glance to my left showed that Giovanni was just above us on the metal platform.

A quick glance was all you could sacrifice when it came to guys like Balthazar.

I'd just register that Giovanni was on the move and seemed to be heading to a set of metal stairs that led down the platform to Jia.

It took a total of two seconds for my brain to process that.

Then in a heartbeat I charged at Balthazar, knocking him to the ground and away from the fucking remote.

My hands on him…

Just touching him gave me a thrill of that sensation of accomplishment. All this time. All these years, all these very long years and I'd never been able to do this.

Just to give him the bone crunching punch I landed straight in his disgusting, fucking face.

All these long years, even before Claire was killed I wanted to do it and as my knuckles connected with his jaw I got the satisfaction I longed for.

Then it hit me, if I killed him, it wouldn't bring her back. The hit was one thing but it wasn't enough. Those long years of seeking vengeance and it wouldn't bring her back, or any of the others. Not my team or the children in the orphanage. It wouldn't change the past.

It was my bad for losing focus because he jabbed me straight in my chest with the end of his gun and something cracked.

Once again I folded and he slipped from under me.

In the split second that he moved he whipped out his gun and aimed it Jia.

I grabbed my gun and shot him but the fucker didn't

go down. The bullet caught his other shoulder and the bastard was still hell bent on going for her.

Then it was like time stood still. I watched him growl like some kind of hell beast, blood dripping from the side of his face, he pulled back the trigger and let it go.

The bullet flew straight at her. Just like Claire. I could have been back there, back in the past and not the present. Distance apart, not close enough.

Jia looked to me, then Giovanni was in front of her.

He'd jumped down from where he was and he was in front of her. In the split of the second I watched the bullet pierce through him stopping the bullet from getting her.

I was sure it went straight into his chest but it didn't take him down.

Balthazar screamed making a hellish sound that reverberated from his fiendish appearance and reached for the remote for the platform.

I shot it out of his hand and didn't give him the chance to come for me again.

As he turned to face me I sent two shots straight into his head.

His mouth opened.

That was it…

He then dropped dead before me.

I killed him.

It's funny I always thought I'd feel better when I did that.

Now that I'd done it, I just wanted to put the past behind me.

I looked over to Jia and Giovanni and realized straight away that this nightmare wasn't over yet.

The platform they were on had started to jerk and was slowly making its way down into the pit of crocs.

Panic filled me and I looked around for the remote only to see it smashed up on the ground across from me.

CHAPTER 21

Jia

As soon as Pa removed the gag from my mouth I screamed out.

The scream poured from me in response not only to the nightmarish creatures surrounding us but Pa too…

The bullet got him. It did. I was sure it hit him.

For a moment I thought maybe it didn't get him. I'd thought maybe he was okay because he was moving around and hadn't fallen. He'd taken the gag away from my mouth and started undoing the ropes securing my feet to the pole.

It was when he stood up to undo the ropes binding

my body and my hands together that I saw the red, red path of blood seeping through his clothes. He'd had on full black with a white t-shirt underneath the black jacket. The shirt couldn't hardly be classed as white anymore.

"Papa, you've been shot," I wailed. Tears poured from my eyes when his hands shook and I could see that he was barely keeping himself together.

"Don't worry about me my bellezza." He stumbled and pulled a knife from his back pocket to slice at the ropes.

Damn it the platform jerked again and I screamed from deep within me as a massive, monstrous crocodile leapt up on to the edge.

That was how close we were now to them.

I hated these creatures so much. I was so terrified my skin crawled and it looked like we were going to be eaten by them.

Pa pulled his gun and shot the one that came up in its head. It flopped back into the water. He fired a few more shots and took out some more.

Once we had a little clearing he returned to undoing the ropes securing me.

Terror made me look around for Xander.

I couldn't see him.

Pa bit down hard on his back teeth, looking pale. My arms loosened on the last cut of the knife and he pulled the rest of the rope away, picking me up like I weighed nothing, but the pain got to him and made him tremble. Still he held me to him and tried to move to the edge of the bridge where he'd come from.

"Pa let me go. I'll help you," I insisted .

"No, Jia, for once in your life listen to me," he balked.

"Pa you've been shot," I shrieked.

He took a moment to look at me and I saw something I'd never seen in him before. It was the end.

I didn't know how to explain it other than that.

It was final and filled with sorrow, regret, deep sadness.

"I'm sorry. This happened because of me. Please remember me cooking for you, and maybe remember this part. All the parts where I was just your father and not the mafia boss. Not the Vegas King. Just your father, bellezza."

"Papa please, don't talk like that. Come I'll help you get up the bridge and we can go to the hospital."

When the platform jerked again and lowered, his face returned to the usual sternness I was used to.

A loud clank made us look up. It was Xander. He'd jumped from a height I didn't know was humanly possible and landed on the suspension bridge. Then he came charging down it towards us, moving lightning fast across the bridge. The damn bridge that was just a little better than walking a tight rope. The little wooden path made into it was just to secure your footing but it still swung like it would just give at any moment.

When Balthazar had brought me out here I didn't know how I didn't die from the sight of the crocodiles and being on the bridge. When I realized his intention was to tied me to the fucking pole in prelude to them eating me, I knew I had bigger problems.

"It's about fucking time," Pa shouted when Xander got to us.

Xander hooked his leg in between one of the wooden wrongs and lowered his body down.

Neither he nor Pa spared any time to say anything further. As Pa hoisted me up to him, Xander reached for me and picked me up, lifting me to safety.

That left Pa though.

Xander set me down next to him and turned around to get Pa who had doubled over.

"Giovanni get here," Xander cried.

My eyes widened as two crocs started making their way up the platform.

Pa slumped, took out his gun and shot them. They flipped over, back into the water but the platform was so low now that the water had started to drift onto it.

"Paaaa, come on please," I cried.

"Xander Cage, remember what I said to you. Take

care of my little girl. Make sure she's safe," Pa replied, glancing at Xander.

Xander wasn't listening. As two more crocs started making their way up to Pa he shot them and fired several more shots at the ones coming.

"Giovanni, you fucking bastard! You think I want my girl to remember her father getting eaten by crocodiles. Get the fuck up now!" Xander wailed and lowered himself even more.

I was crying so much I couldn't see, but something sparked inside me when Pa stood up, turned to us and reached up.

Hope filled me and Xander grabbed his hands with what looked like all his strength and pulled Pa up. He pulled him up and dragged him the rest of the way up on to the bridge.

Just as he did so the platform went straight down into the water and the remaining crocs just swam around it. Another second and that would have been it we wouldn't have had a choice.

"Let's get out of here," Xander said to me. A slight brush of his fingers on my cheek soothed my soul.

A look at Pa though drained me.

He looked paler and weary. So weary and weak.

I nodded and moved forward, while Xander helped Pa.

Pa started coughing when we got to the entrance that took us back to the corridor.

Being on an actual floor allowed us to move faster.

However, when we turned the corridor Pa's legs gave and he pulled out of Xander's hold. I stopped my flight and moved back to them.

Pa shook his head at me, grabbed his chest and slumped down to the ground with his back against the wall. There was so much blood now.

I looked to Xander. His face was filled with the doom I felt. As were his eyes.

It was like he knew what was going to happen next. I did too, but I didn't want it to.

I returned my focus to Pa and he shook his head again.

He reached out to cup my face and pulled me closer to plant a kiss on my forehead.

"It's okay. It's going to be okay," Pa said in a frail voice. "I'm sorry I won't see you become who you wanted to be. Bellezza, you'll be a great artist. One of the finest."

"You gave me my first paint set." I smiled.

"Yes, and what a good idea that was. Follow your dreams Jia. Follow your heart, bellezza." He gave me a weak smile and looked to Xander. "Please just get her out of here and make sure she's safe. She's the most important thing to me."

Xander crouched down next to Pa and nodded.

"I will, she's the most important thing to me too. She will be safe as long as I live."

Pa's hands dropped from my face. He reached for Xander's shirt and nodded.

"That's more than I could hope for … Ace."

When he set his head back against the wall, his eyes became glassy and a tear trailed down the corner of is cheek.

"Pa, please don't leave me. I love you."

"I love you too, Jia. I will always be here." He placed his hand on his heart , looked at me and then it was like something switched off inside him.

I sucked in a sharp breath and the tears pour from inside my soul.

As I looked at my father I saw him as my father. not the person who'd done so much wrong. Not that man who terrified me with all the ways he could shock me. It was the first time that he didn't look like a monster.

"Papa…" I touched his cheek which now started to feel cold.

Xander placed his arm around me and I looked to him.

"Xander… my father…"

"I know I –"

Footsteps echoed down the hall. It was only the sound that snapped me back to reality. We were still in this place. The Ra were still very much at work and I didn't think it mattered that Balthazar was dead.

The instinct to flee washed over me, but... how could I leave Pa?

How could I leave Pa here?

"Jia, listen to me, we have to get out of here now. We have to."

"I can't leave him here like this." I shook my head. "I can't Xander. I can't just leave him."

He tightened his grip on me and gazed deeply into my eyes. "I just promised your father I'd take care of you and keep you safe. I promised him Jia. I promised him. Please let me do that. Please *allow* me to do that."

My shoulders tensed and I nodded realizing I didn't have much time to think.

The footsteps were getting closer and were now accompanied by voices. It was definitely some of the men here. I could tell.

I stood up and Xander took my hand. One last look at Pa and we left. As soon as I moved numbness filled my body.

I ran as fast as I could with Xander next to me. We got to a path that led down a staircase. It was still part of the factory style set up but rougher looking like no one ever came out back here.

We went down to where the drains were and then it all changed to a tunnel like passage.

No one was chasing us but we were still going.

A light appeared ahead of us and I prayed it was daylight.

We got closer and my heart soared when I saw that it really was daylight. Sunlight streamed through the panels leading into the tunnels.

We went outside and the air filled my lungs.

I cast my gaze around me and saw that the situation was in hand.

Surrounding us was what I called an army.

It looked like the whole US army had come in to help.

Xander lowered his gun but kept hold of me.

It was over.

All of it was over and Pa was dead.

The thought brought the tears back and I broke down when Xander pulled me into his chest. Close to his heart.

CHAPTER 22

Jia

Six months later ...

I finished up the last strokes on the oil painting I'd done of the beach in Tuscany.

It looked just as I'd remembered it and I was happy with the work I'd done.

It was one of the places my parents used to take me on vacation when I was little. We had some happy memories there on the beach.

We'd spent hours on the beach just enjoying the way everything looked. It was there that I'd first decided I was going to be an artist. I was nine and I was so happy that I'd found my thing in life that I'd wanted to do.

I went back with Xander twice in the last few months. The first time was just for the sake of going back and to show him one of the places I treasured. We stayed in the beach house I always stayed at with my family. While I hadn't been back in years I fell in love with the house and the place all over again. Just like the first time Pa took Ma and me there. The place reminded me of some kind of fairytale. Or a dream.

The next time Xander and I went was his doing.

The man never ceased to amaze me. It was for my birthday. A birthday trip that turned into something that healed me because I realized I had him. I really did.

For my birthday, Xander bought the house and asked me to move in with him.

That was what he did.

That was last month. When we got back I decided I'd do this painting. I was taking my time with it.

Like always painting provided the escape I needed whenever my thoughts were unsettled. The last few months had been beautiful for Xander and me but they were also hard.

"Is there anything else I can do before I go?" Anya asked pulling me from my thoughts.

My best friend had been my rock for the last six months. She'd barely left my side. *Barely*, and only when Xander was around. It was only then that she'd take her leave and honestly he was just as bad.

She'd come by to spend the day with me.

"I'll be fine Anya. Go have fun with Tim." I turned away from my easel and gave her a mischievous smile. She'd gone outside to talk with him over an hour ago. That was why I thought I'd spend the time painting.

She started blushing and ran a hand through her hair.

"Oh my gosh. I didn't mean to be gone for so long."

"It's okay. You didn't have to break away from your phone sex to come check on little old me." I giggled. That was me trying to be me.

"We weren't having phone sex." She shook her head and came over to sit on the little wooden chair next to me.

"Weren't you?"

"Not just now." She smiled wide.

She and Tim, who were very serious about each other had a date last night and I knew she felt guilty for not seeing me. I wished she wouldn't though. I knew she was meant to be going somewhere with him today but rearranged so she could see me.

Xander was doing some stuff with Wes and Jack so I would have had the house to myself. It wasn't a bad thing. Everyone however had decided that leaving me alone was off the table. I understood why.

I literally fell apart after Pa died.

For months I wasn't myself. there was rarely a minute that saw me without tears in my eyes. Every day was hard. It was only in the last few months... maybe the last two months that I started to resemble something like myself.

Anya turned and grabbed the bowl of candy she'd shared out earlier when she got here. It was one of those party sized serving bowls. Earlier it was full, now it had gone down to more than half.

I rolled my eyes at myself and reached in for a tootsie roll.

"Good, it's half the fat if we share it," she bubbled.

I lifted my shoulders into a sassy shrug. The seriousness returned to her face when I popped the candy into my mouth.

"You sure you're okay?" she asked. "Jia you know I worry about you."

"You don't have to, and I really hope you're going to see Tim later."

She nodded. "I am, we're gonna go to dinner. I'll leave when Xander gets back."

"Or you could go before and get some time to yourself."

"But, you know I'm going to pass on that so I can make sure I hand you over to the safety of that amazing man of yours." She quirked a brow. "You won't get rid of me so easy, plus I brought the sweets and I'm actively making sure you have enough serotonin to bring out the happy."

I had to laugh. "You are so funny Anya. You really are."

"I'm serious though. I know it's been hard. Every time I think about how hard it's been for you I remember when I felt so helpless. Every time I felt helpless and it was like there was nothing I could do to help you. It's been three major times now. Your mom's death, going to Italy with Armand and your father's death."

I looked at her and I understood.

We were as close as sisters could be. She was definitely that for me. I'd known her for so long and we'd gone through life together. I knew what she meant about feeling helpless. I knew if the tables had been turned I would have felt the same as her.

I reached over and took both her hands into mine.

"Anya, you may have felt helpless but your presence was what I needed. That was all. That was all I needed, just to have you. You did all you could do for me by just being there. You're here now."

She gave me a curt nod. "Thank you, and please humor me a little longer so I can just know you'll be fine tonight. I rejoice every day that you didn't end up with Armand. I just wish things could have turned out different all around."

"Me too."

Me too indeed.

I wished Pa didn't die.

The grief that had taken hold of me after was indescribable. No one had ever seen me in that state. What they didn't know was that I'd gotten like that as a result of everything.

What kept me going was Xander.

He was my good thing that came out of the darkness.

Between him and Anya they helped me find myself.

And, I had to do that part fast because Pa left me everything. Absolutely everything.

My father left me the whole empire that needed my attention. Things to restructure and sort out.

Everything in Vegas, Italy and the other property development businesses in L.A and New York.

Everything: all is assets and people. The knights stayed together and became mine. All except Armand who'd been incarcerated for the last six months. Who I relied on a lot to help me run the place was Frankie.

I put him in charge of everything. When I could I went to The Grand Marchesi probably once every other week. It was just to check in on the place. It was all I could stand to bear since it was weird not seeing Pa around. Or feeling his strong presence.

Frankie became my right hand man, and truthfully he was more like the boss. He did a lot for me. A lot I never knew about and honestly, a lot I didn't want to know. I asked him and Vinny to clean up and sort out all the dirty dealings.

They'd know what to do and what I meant.

There was enough wealth to take care of everything. I wasn't going to fall prey to greed and want after more. I guess I was the boss now and had a multi-billion-dollar fortune of countless wealth untold and the people that came with it.

What I valued most of all was my freedom.

That came too with deciding what happened next.

That part was where I was at. I was finally ready to do more with my life.

Anya grabbed some more sweets and beamed from ear to ear just as we heard the door downstairs open.

That would be the amazing man of mine. It was eight and he was here just as he promised. He was like clockwork and as reliable as the sun.

My stomach still did that little flutter when I knew I was going to see him.

In the mornings though, when I woke up in his arms, it was more of a tingle that flushed over my whole being.

"You should see your face." Anya giggled getting up.

Heat crept into my cheeks. "I'm just happy to see him."

"I can see that."

Xander appeared at the door looking as handsome as ever. The sight of him brought an instant smile to my face.

"Girls, everything okay here?" he asked grinning back at me.

"You know it is." Anya beamed then waved her hand at him. "I will see you guys later."

She bent down to give me a hug then sauntered away with a bounce in her step.

As she walked out Xander approached me and I stood when he got up to me, falling into his embrace. I loved resting my head on his wide powerful chest.

I lifted my head though so I could kiss him.

"How's my girl?"

"She's good now that her man is home." I loved saying that. The house had instantly felt like a home when he moved in. Then our place in Italy felt like where my heart wanted to be when we were there together.

I tried to figure out the distinction then I realized there wasn't one. It was him.

That was the answer.

Home was where ever he was.

"How's my man?" I asked kissing the edge of his cheek.

"Finally ready to get life on track with his girl."

I liked the sound of that. I knew it meant more though since he'd seen Jack and Wes today. For this whole time he'd been with me supporting me and hadn't done much for himself.

We lived together here, we had a home in Italy, and we were planning to go there in a few weeks so that I could continue my studies. That was as much as I knew in regards to us. Except that was all about me.

He pulled me into his lap as he sat on the chair and slipped his arm around my waist.

His expression looked like he had much to tell.

"I'm telling you this because I've thought about a lot and decided what I want to do," he began.

"It sounds all secret." I smiled.

"It's supposed to be, but I won't keep secrets from you. SMF want me back. They asked me to come back over a month ago and gave me time to think about it."

I gasped. "Xander, over a month?"

"Yeah, it's cool baby. I took the time because I knew I was going to say no." His gaze clung to mine.

"You said no?"

He nodded. "I said no. I loved being an agent. I loved getting to use my skills for good. But that feels like a part of me that no longer exists. I don't think I want that life anymore and it would mean keeping secrets from you. I wouldn't even be able to tell you that I work there. I don't want that."

I cupped his chin. "What do you want Xander? Tell me. I'll be with you a hundred percent."

"I want you."

I laughed. "Your sweet."

"I'm serious. I want you. I want a life with you. That was the first thing I decided. It was true to me and when I thought of what I want with you I followed the other path."

"What path is this?"

"The path where I'll be working with Jack, Wes and Dorian as a consultancy."

My gosh I remembered Jack talking about this with Frankie. In the end of the crazy saga with The Ra it was Jack who was able to summon a hundred marines who took out and shut down the secret facility. It showed the extent of his influence and power, so I knew it was no mere consultancy Xander was talking about.

"That sounds good, but is it dangerous?"

"No, just intel. That's all. No chasing anybody. Best of all I'll probably do a few jobs a year and we can live in Italy if that's what you want."

"Oh my God." My spirits lifted. "You mean it?"

"Yeah. I mean I know you won't just want to be there the whole time so we can travel backwards and forwards, just be there more. Live there. If that's what you want. That's why I bought the house."

It wasn't until the tear splashed on to my lap that I realized I was crying and quickly wiped the rest away.

"You are too much Mister. I want that, but only if you want it. I know you've been doing a lot of what I want and I love you for that. I really do. I want you to be happy too."

"Told you what I want Jia. I mean it. I'm the kind of guy who doesn't need to be grounded anywhere to do what I want to do. I have Jack and Wes and we'll be working together. That's me done and I'm happy with my decision. It's what I want and I have to say Italy rubbed off on me too."

I laughed. "It's so beautiful Xander. I never really thought of living there because I knew it would get on my father's nerves but I think my heart is there. So much bad happened here."

"I know. So how about a fresh start? You and me Bellezza." The blue hue of his eyes sparkled with the hope I felt rippling within me.

"Yes. I absolutely love that. A new start with you."

He leaned forward and pressed his forehead to mine.

EPILOGUE

Xander

FOUR MONTHS LATER...

The beautiful Tuscan sky was almost as beautiful as Jia.

The sight of both was enough to steal my breath away.

She was walking up from the beach toward the house. The sun was low, just getting ready to set and it cast her in that brilliant glow , enhancing her ethereal beauty.

"Xander, you still there?" Wes asked.

I pressed the phone to my ear as I refocused on our conversation.

I must have paused for a good minute as I'd watched Jia walk up the path.

"Sorry yeah. I gotta go though buddy." I chuckled.

Wes was talking work and I would be no good to him with my mind like this. I got the gist of the job. We were investigating a U.S general. He'd started talking about the job specs when I zoned out and my mind decided it would grab the details when I saw Wes and Jack next month.

It might be something I may have to bow out of though if it got as strenuous as the last job because I had something else planned that was going to take up the next few months.

Maybe three or four. It depended.

That plan was more important than the job.

"I just started talking to you," Wes complained. I could almost imagine him rolling his eyes at me.

He shouldn't because he was just as loved up as me when it came to his woman.

I was just more open about it. Like I was going to be now.

"My girl just came back and I need her." I smiled.

"Oh my God Xander… you make me sick. One year and you are the same."

Yup, one year. Last week was exactly a year since I'd known Jia. A year ago all the shit with Giovanni went down, secrets spilled out into the open and lies were uncovered.

Fuck.

One year and it had been quite the year.

But, the good part of it was just walking through the door of our home and she smiled when she looked at me.

"I'll be the same for the next million years." I nodded with a surety even though he couldn't see me.

"Okay pal, call me when you can."

"Sure." I hung up and gave my undivided attention to my girl as she skipped into my arms, and pressed her lips to mine.

The kiss she gave me was like coming home and the type of hunger that consumed me made me want to devour her.

That was exactly what I planned to do. Devour her, here in our paradise home where she was all mine and she had all of me.

It was us.

She felt true to me. Everything that we were as a couple felt like what I'd wanted most. She felt true to me because we both looked out for each other, wanted each other's happiness, and she healed my heart. She'd healed me and breathed new life into me. That was why I took the consultancy job with Jack and Wes.

Everything all worked out and now I was looking forward to the next chapter of our lives.

I swooped her up and headed up to our bedroom. My lips never leaving hers for a second. Not even for a breath.

I set her down in the center of the bed and we kissed the clothes off each other.

Wild and raw, but sensual. That was us.

I'd never experienced anything like it. She was like a drug to me.

I craved her more and more every time I was with her. Every second of every day. Every minute.

I didn't know it was possible to feel this way. Different to how I'd been with anybody, not just Claire.

It was different and I knew I was one damn lucky guy to have what I had with Jia.

I might not be the most romantic person. I might not have come from the most loving background but I believed that you knew true love when you found it.

It was what I had now.

I kissed and tasted her all over, loving the sight of her writhe against the pleasure I gave her with my mouth. My lips showing her how I adored every part of her body.

Her lips on mine, my lips on her neck, her breasts, her tight taught pink nipples, the valley between her breasts and the flat plane of her stomach, right down to her pretty pussy.

Her body welcomed me as I plunged into her, searing into her with the length of my cock, making her mine all over again.

Mine.

I meant every word I'd said when I told her I wanted her. She was what I wanted. She was what I needed. Only she could do this to me. Make me get lost in passion.

It called to both of us and we answered.

The carnal rhythm that took us sent me over the edge of reason and reality.

Lost and trapped in passions force and will, we moved together.

Me pumping into her and her moving her hips against me in the same wild way showing me that she wanted me too.

I already knew we wouldn't last long going at that pace. It would only be a matter of time before we burned right the hell out. Burnt, scorched clean.

The burn out came as we climaxed.

We both cried out from the intensity and she arched into my chest, head pressing back into the pillows as she came. The walls of her sweet pussy tightened around my cock like a vise and the orgasm finished me off too.

We were both breathing hard.

Breathing so hard I couldn't catch my breath. I'd just caught it when she reached up to kiss me. That just made me want her all over again.

"I love you," she breathed against my lips.

Every time she said those words it got me, because I remembered the first time I told her and how I wished it could have been under different circumstances. I remembered how I nearly died at her father's hand and how I wished I could have one more chance to tell her how I felt.

Every chance I'd gotten since then was beautiful.

Now was no different. Except now the question I planned to ask her in a few days slipped into my mind.

"I love you Jia." I nuzzled my nose against hers.

It was time now. I couldn't wait for a few days or another minute.

The same way you knew when you had true love, the same way you knew when you should do something as important as what I was about to.

I moved away from her and she pretended to pout, then reached back for me.

"No, there's no way you're going back on that call to Wes or whoever." She giggled.

"There's no way Wes or whoever will have any of my attention with you around."

"Then come back here. I want more," she purred and a hum of satisfaction slipped from her lips when I ran my fingers over the tight creamy skin of her stomach.

"You'll get more," I promised. "I have something to ask you."

"Yes." She nodded vigorously and I laughed.

"Baby you don't know what I'm going to ask you."

"Whatever it is, it's a yes from me." She pulled the sheet over her breasts and sat up nestling her hair over her shoulder.

I hoped it was yes.

I pulled my boxers back on deciding I'd do this properly, even in my limited clothing. The original plan was at the restaurant on the beach she loved surrounded by candlelight.

This felt better.

Jia looked on in curiosity as I moved to the night stand and pulled out a little velvet box.

She didn't see the box properly until I came around to her side of the bed. Then she bolted up and her mouth dropped open.

I got down on one knee and she covered her mouth.

"Xander…"

"Yes, baby."

"What are you doing? I mean it looks like you're doing something and I think I know what it is, but

please don't let that be another necklace. Not that I
didn't love the last necklace."

She always babbled when she got nervous and her
cheeks would flush with that soft rose color.

"What do you want it to be?" I decided to tease.

She shook her head and blinked. "The thing my
heart wants the most."

"What's that?"

"You."

Thank God for that.

I snapped the box open and she brought her hands
closer to her heart when her beautiful eyes saw the
princess cut diamond ring I had made for her. Anya
helped me design it.

When I decided I'd do this I couldn't think of
anyone better to take ring shopping.

From the look of Jia I could tell I'd done the right
thing. her eyes brimmed with tears.

"Xander…"

I took her hand and held it. "Jia… I've said you've
had me from hello and I meant that. I promised your
father I'd take care of you but I always planned to do
that. I dreamed of us having happy days together, the
kind you get lost in. But lost in the way you feel because
it's so unreal. I had a lot of years where I was lost in the
worse of ways. Lost in darkness. Then I found you and

you had me lost in you. Lost in love with you. No one compares to you. It would be the greatest honor and privilege to me, if you were my wife. Please be mine."

I might not be the best romantic, but that sounded pretty damn good to me. My heart took over and did it all. It spoke to her, speaking words from my soul and everything that made me, me.

My heart sored when she nodded.

"Yes… of course it's a yes." She cupped my face. "I was lost too and then I found you. I was right there with you lost in love. But you did more for me. You saved me in so many ways, Xander Cage. You saved me and it's me who is honored and privileged to have you. Thank you for not giving up on me when you could have."

"That was never going to happen." I nodded firmly and slipped the ring on her finger.

We both looked at it and she held it up. The diamond sparkled against the light and she laughed.

She laughed and threw her arms around me.

When our lips met for another kiss everything felt different.

It felt more like we belonged to each other.

But… we always did.

Always… right from hello.

She was always the queen of my heart.

Thanks so much for reading.
I hope you enjoyed Xander and Jia's story.

ABOUT THE AUTHOR

Khardine Gray is an USA Today Bestselling author.

She writes contemporary romance and romantic suspense.

Her books have sexy, drool-worthy heroes who will make you melt, and sassy, fun loving, ambitious heroines.

She simply adores her readers and loves spoiling them.

Keep up with all her new releases by signing up to her mailing list at:

Connect with Khardine on Facebook in her reader group-

The Bliss Romance Hideaway readers group - https://www.facebook.com/ groups/889377571219117/

Amazon-

https://www.amazon.com/ author/khardinegraynovels

Bookbub

https://www.bookbub.com/authors/khardine-gray

Mailing list

https://www. subscribepage.com/khardinegraybooks

ACKNOWLEDGMENTS